The Body
And Its Dangers

Stonewall Inn Editions

Buddies by Ethan Mordden
Joseph and the Old Man by Christopher Davis
Blackbird by Larry Duplechan
Gay Priest by Malcolm Boyd
Privates by Gene Horowitz
Taking Care of Mrs. Carroll by Paul Monette
Conversations with My Elders by Boze Hadleigh
Epidemic of Courage by Lon Nungesser
One Last Waltz by Ethan Mordden
Gay Spirit by Mark Thompson, ed.
As If After Sex by Joseph Torchia
The Mayor of Castro Street by Randy Shilts
Nocturnes for the King of Naples by Edmund White
Alienated Affections by Seymour Kleinberg
Sunday's Child by Edward Phillips
God of Ecstasy by Arthur Evans
Valley of the Shadow by Christopher Davis
Love Alone by Paul Monette
The Boys and Their Baby by Larry Wolff
On Being Gay by Brian McNaught
Parisian Lives by Samuel M. Steward
Living the Spirit by Will Roscoe, ed.
Everybody Loves You by Ethan Mordden
Untold Decades by Robert Patrick
Gay and Lesbian Poetry in Our Time by Carl Morse
  and Joan Larkin, eds.
Reports from the holocaust by Larry Kramer
Personal Dispatches by John Preston, ed.
Tangled Up in Blue by Larry Duplechan
How to Go to the Movies by Quentin Crisp
Just Say No by Larry Kramer
The Prospect of Detachment by Lindsley Cameron
The Body and Its Dangers and Other Stories by Allen Barnett

Stonewall Inn Mysteries

Death Takes the Stage by Donald Ward
Sherlock Holmes and the Mysterious Friend of Oscar Wilde
  by Russell A. Brown
A Simple Suburban Murder by Mark Richard Zubro
A Body to Dye For by Grant Michaels
Why Isn't Becky Twitchell Dead? by Mark Richard Zubro

THE BODY
AND ITS
DANGERS
=
And Other Stories

ALLEN BARNETT

ST. MARTIN'S PRESS
New York

"Philostorgy, Now Obscure" originally appeared, in substantially different form, in *The New Yorker.* Copyright © Allen Barnett 1990.

"Snapshot" was first published in *Christopher Street* magazine, May 1986.

Library of Congress Cataloging-in-Publication Data

Barnett, Allen.
     The body and its dangers and other stories / Allen Barnett.
          p.   cm. — (Stonewall Inn editions)
     ISBN 0-312-05824-1 (pbk.)
     1. Gay men—Fiction.   I. Title.   II. Series.
     PS3552.A6965B64   1991
     813'.54—dc20   90-28375
                                                                            CIP

First U.S. Paperback Edition: July 1991
10 9 8 7 6 5 4 3 2 1

Acknowledgments

I must acknowledge two books that were especially helpful in writing the story "Succor." These are Georgina Masson's *The Companion Guide to Rome* and Anya M. Shetterly's *Romewalks*. When in Rome, do as they do. Elaine Pagel's *Adam, Eve, and the Serpent* was a great trampoline of ideas, especially as I was writing, and rewriting, the two "Body" stories.

I was about to give up writing altogether when I received an unexpected windfall from The New York Foundation for the Arts, plus the publication of my story "Snapshot" by Charles Ortleb and Tom Steele in *Christopher Street* magazine. They have published writers no one else would. I am grateful for the encouragement of Herbert H. Breslin, Sandra McCormack, and most of all, Michael Denneny. I am very proud that he is my editor.

Contents

Occasionally, characters in these stories are named after friends who have died of Acquired Immune Deficiency Syndrome. I do not mean to imply any similarity between the real person and the fictional; this was an attempt to keep them alive in my imagination, to keep the pleasure of their company as long as I could sustain it. Jay Frank and Robert Mazzochi, I think, would be delighted to know their names were used in such a fashion.

There are other men whose influence, if not their names, affected me as I was writing. I wish to remember, now and always, these very decent and lovely men: Ken Wein, Diego Lopez, Luis Palacios-Jimenez, Paul Rappaport, and Peter Kunz Opfersei. It is impossible to follow in the footsteps of the dead.

If I could reach you now, in any way
At all, I would say this to you . . .

      —*Thomas James*

SNAPSHOT

=

There is something I do not like about old photographs—
snapshots, I should say—the kind that one's grandmother
keeps in a box on a closet shelf, or in old albums that crack as
the black pages are turned, spilling more photos than are held
in place. I don't like the way the people in these photographs
speak in a tense that is theirs alone, or their unquestioning
faith in the present tense. Now, the smiling person seems to
say, Should I sit on the couch or the coffee table? Should I
hold the baby? Should I hold my knee? Yes! Now!—this is
me at my best. I do not like the way these old pictures fail the

trust that is placed in them. I do not like how easily we are betrayed, or how easily we betray ourselves.

When I was seven my mother showed me a snapshot of a young soldier standing at ease in front of a building made of corrugated iron. The photographer and his Brownie were too far away from the subject—the soldier's face was nothing but a squint against the sun.

"This is your real father," my mother told me. "Dale is not your daddy, honey, and never was. You don't have to love him." On the back of the snapshot was printed Kodak 1954.

"That boy will grow up hating you and him both," my grandmother said, with her face in the bulge of the screen door, referring to the man in the photo. She was a woman with black and white convictions, and a mouth that seemed weighted at the corners, especially when she smiled.

"He will hate me more if he finds out for himself," my mother replied, implying that I would hate her, either/or.

My grandmother stepped back into the house and my mother went in after her. "Illegitimate," I heard my grandmother say. I didn't know what the word meant, but I knew its reference was to me, for it was always said to imply that I hadn't been sufficiently punished for something, or that I was spoiled and in some way responsible for my mother's state of affairs, which had never been much good.

I went to sit on the curb to get away from this adult conversation and its implications, which made me feel self-conscious and imperiled. We lived in what my mother called a subdivision, in a cracker-box house on a slab of cement. If you fell on the floor and cracked your head, it could be heard out on the street. Up and down May Street, the houses were identical to ours, distinguished only by the upkeep of the lawn, or the color of the stamped-sheet, tar-paper shingles that covered each house.

It was early summer and the curb was filled with drifts of shiny black cinders that had been spread there over the winter.

Hiding on the other side of the house across the street was a teenaged girl staring up into the eyes of her boyfriend. Her mother came to the screen door often, looking up and down the street for her daughter to come in and set the table. It was five-thirty and time to eat; her dad and everyone else's dad was home from the factory, but she remained in the bed of petunias, flowers that have always reminded me of girls who wear too much makeup and cheap fabrics because they don't know any better.

A group of children rode by on their bicycles, and a grief rose up in me like the kind of nausea that overwhelms without any kind of warning, and which I struggled—unsuccessfully —to keep down. It was also that hour of the day when the petunias smelled like the lady's counter at the shopping center Walgreen's, and unseen clouds of their scent hovered at the level of my face, dizzying as a kitchen filled with cigarette smoke and adult laughter.

"Honey, why are you crying?" my mother asked with enough self-blame in her voice to hurt the both of us. I was not a particularly sensitive child, and I seldom wept. My mother's shadow was stretching long and thin into the street. I wanted to tell her, For no reason, for no reason at all—the way she would answer me when I walked in on her and found her crying into a ball of tissue for no apparent reason. But something urgent was beating at the base of my skull: You, you, you.

"I don't know how to ride a bicycle," I cried.

She sat down next to me on the curb. She put her head down and covered her face with one hand. Her shoulders trembled. I stopped crying then.

Unoriginal as this may sound, it occurred to me as we sat on the curb of a street of identical houses that there were probably a good dozen other moon-faced kids hiding on the side of the house from their mothers in this subdivision alone, that there could be as many other seven-year-olds who could not ride a bicycle or swim, sitting with dusty sneakers in the cinders beside their beautiful young mothers, who were themselves sitting there crying at the pain and failure of everything they had ever done.

This little scene repeated itself over and over in my head, as if we sat between two mirrors, nothing at all unique about us, and felt like the solution that, once found, turns a puzzle into a used toy. If it was not completely comforting, this vision, it did give the world a kind of balance, or at least tipped the scales in my favor, and I wouldn't have to think about myself so much. There is a school of thought that says children know more than they let on, but I am willing to concede that I knew nothing at all.

My mother divorced Dale, married again a year later, and her second husband adopted me when I was thirteen. At the arrival of my new birth certificate in the mail, my mother said, "No one will ever be able to prove that he isn't your real father," as if this would be a point of pride or contention, I wasn't sure. Anyone looking at us could tell that we were not related. He looked like a prince from a picture book. We didn't love one another, but we could talk out of a mutual, if casual, curiosity. When I turned seventeen, they bought me a used Volkswagen.

Teaching me how to use the clutch, alone on a country road, he said, "I've always wanted to ask . . . do you ever miss your real father?"

Inside the dim light of the car, the headlights just grazing freshly plowed fields, I imagined we could be the subject of a magazine ad. "His first car. There are things you've never talked about. Aren't you glad it's a Volkswagen?"

"How could I miss someone I never knew?"

"Do you want to know him?"

"I don't even know his name."

"Don't you ever want to tell him about yourself?" he asked with uncharacteristic concern. "Don't you think he wants to know? He is your father."

"No, really. I don't think of him as my father." I told him the truth and I told him what I thought he wanted to hear.

"Turn around."

"What?"

"Just turn around at this farm."

I drove us home and he jumped out of the car even before it came to a stop.

I didn't think about this evening until six years later when he and my mother were divorcing. He had already moved to Denver and I was packing to move to Thunderbird, Arizona, to get my M.B.A.

"Do you think you'll ever see him again?" my mother asked.

"I will not go looking for him, if that's what you mean."

"You were always a mother's boy," she said. "That's probably my fault."

"The adoption wasn't my idea," I told her. "You just wanted you and me to have the same name."

"Is that so bad?" she asked.

"The only time he wanted to know what I thought about anything was the night I got the Volkswagen. He asked me if I ever wanted to know my real father."

"I remember that night," she said. "He got drunk and cried himself to sleep."

"Him drunk? Really?" He and my mother drank only on Christmas and New Year's Eve. A bottle of gin lasted them three years.

"He had a daughter, you know. From a previous marriage. His wife got custody of the little girl and then skipped state. She never wrote, never called, and he didn't have the money to go looking for them. The last he heard, his wife had married well and her second husband adopted the kid. He still carries a snapshot of her in his wallet. I think that's the saddest thing."

Sentimentality in my mother always surprised me, for she had had many illusions shattered at an early age. She stood and walked away from me in a graceful but masculine manner. Her pose at the sink reminded me of her recent husband, the man who adopted me, an attitude he would take when he was talking about plans for the house or lecturing me about Vietnam and duty to one's country. It occurred to me that he was legally still my father despite the divorce, and I wondered whether there would ever be an incident in which I would be called back into his life. Was I responsible for him in case of accident or old age? Would someone call me if he died without a will? I wondered whether there wasn't an expiration date on relationships like these.

I considered the color-coordinated kitchen, the pot holders hanging from the refrigerator by hidden magnets, all the evidence that the two of them had worked hard enough to ascend tentatively into the middle class. I was going after an M.B.A. to make that ascendancy all the more secure. If anyone had asked me what I wanted from life, I would have replied, Quality. I wanted to be able to assume my right to things.

My mother asked, "Don't you ever want to know the circumstances of your birth?"

I went to the kitchen door. "No," I said, telling her the truth because I didn't know what she wanted to hear. "You make it sound as if there was criminal activity involved."

"In some states, there would have been," she said, and picked at something caught in her teeth with a matchbook cover.

Out the door, I looked across the backyard. It ended at a high-voltage tower, beyond which there once had been a cornfield, which was beautiful; then soybeans, which were not. Then one year nothing was planted. Weeds grew in the fertile ground as high as a woman's head. There was nothing in the field then. It was supposed to be a park, but it was only an ugly spread of short, stubby, hard grass. I was just about to walk out the door to get away from my mother's gaze for a moment when she said, "I don't want you to blame me."

"As a matter of fact," I said, "I have always blamed myself." Then I broke into a sudden and foolish laughter.

"That's ridiculous."

"Nevertheless."

"You can't take responsibility for your own birth."

"Nevertheless," I repeated, still laughing. It was preposterous and absolutely true, and the recognition of this fact made me feel light-headed and released, like a balloon detached from a child's hand. My mother had more to say, but I wasn't letting her. I was comfortable, isolated, floating away.

But when I arrived in Arizona the next day, I opened a suitcase and found three old letters and a snapshot of my mother. On the back of the snapshot was written, "Lorraine to Joe. October 1954. Union City, Tenn." My mother's hair in the photo was very long, bleached blond and parted down the side like Veronica Lake's. She was braced on the arm of a large sofa, legs crossed like a man's, smiling directly at the person for whom the snapshot was obviously intended. It was easy to imagine even from the black and white picture that the color of her lips was bright red. Her bravura was touching—fifteen years old and pregnant with me.

The three envelopes were postmarked Fort Leonard Wood, Missouri, an army base, dated the September and October of the year before I was born, and sent to Union City, Tennessee. They were from a Private Joseph James.

"Joe wanted to marry me," she said. "It was his mother who made him join the army. I took the bus from Michigan to Tennessee so we could be together. There was a bar in Union City where my dad used to sing before he married your grandmother. They gave me a job because they thought I was your Aunt Esther. The picture I gave you was taken in the little apartment they gave me right above the bar."

I felt leaden, weighted, stilled: the feeling you get when a blanket that has been tossed over you descends, then is tucked up to your chin. I had only called to tell her I had arrived safely in Thunderbird. She wanted to tell me everything, and everything she wanted to tell me required my wanting to know. She must have felt that she had no claim on me as a mother if she could not tell me the truth I was supposed to desire. For my part, it was like being the object of longing by someone who loves you too much and wants to tell you everything in hope that that will make you love them more. Under this pressure, I was the one to acquiesce and I asked the requisite questions, but only like an uninvolved stage manager rehearsing an actress who has trouble with her lines.

"Why didn't you marry Joe in Tennessee?"

"Because people figured out where I was, and his mother sent him a letter telling him he couldn't marry me until he was out of the army. You would have been almost four years old by then. Joe wrote to tell me what she said and I got so mad I tore the letter up and wrote back to tell him not to worry about marrying me. I told him I was already married. And I signed the letter Mrs. Ernest Wray."

"Who was that?"

"He was a very nice old man who bought my bus ticket back to Michigan and sent you a blue blanket when you were born. I went to work at the Victory Grill, the truck stop where I met Dale."

"And why'd you marry him?"

"He was kind to me, bought me cigarettes, and didn't mind that I already had a baby. What choices did I have?"

I had by this time only a vague memory of the man she married instead of my real father: the thickness of his hair, the shape of his nose, the kind of clothes he wore. We saw him only when he was moving us from one place to another, dark basement apartments in marginal neighborhoods, or those war-built housing developments in factory towns that spread during the baby boom like measles among schoolchildren. Dale had been one of the first of the successful truck drivers in the years when highways were replacing the railroads, but my mother and I were dependent upon bags of groceries from neighbors, upon landlords who would wait for their rent check while Dale was on the road for weeks at a time. So my memory of him was like an allergy you don't get until you are older, and suddenly your head fills up, your tongue swells, your eyes burn, or your skin breaks out in reaction to something that you've been eating all your life.

"Why did you give me these letters?" I asked her.

"In case you wanted to go looking for Joe, he couldn't deny who you are."

"These are your letters," I said to her, meaning that I did not want them.

The tone of her voice bottomed out, "But I saved them for you!"

"Where is he now?" I asked, for she must have wanted me to, although it seemed as if I knew all this already without knowing how.

"He moved back to Michigan after his service and got married. I was going to give you his letters on your sixteenth birthday, but you never seemed much interested, and it was about that time when Esther called to tell me—she used to tell me whenever she saw him—that Joe's two little girls had been found molested and murdered in a vineyard behind their house. They couldn't have been more than ten or eleven years old. No one ever found out who did it, not even a clue. Esther sent me the clippings from the papers, even the Detroit ones. I saved all of them for you, too, just in case you ever wanted them."

There was a long pause, then she asked, "Are you mad at me for not telling you sooner?"

"No, Mom," I murmured. "How could I be mad?"

"Do you ever think about writing him? You have a right to, you know," he said, his hand on my stomach, envious of how tightly my body held to its youth.

"A right to?" I repeated. "No, really, I never thought of it as something I was entitled to do. Other people find the idea of reaching him more intriguing than I do."

"If you were my son, I would want to hear from you," he said.

"If I were your son? Me, you mean? Not someone else?"

He placed one leg through both of mine and pulled me up close to him back to chest, and said, "When we're in bed together like this, I like to imagine that you are."

We had met when he was looking for someone to take care of his cats while he was in Miami conducting a Broadway-bound musical, and while I was looking for an apartment. I was in New York, where I had been hired at an advertising agency. I did well from the start and got the campaign for a toothpaste that I had been using all my life. His show closed before I found a place of my own. Although our living arrangement was meant to be only temporary, this confession allowed me to think that he wanted me to stay.

Also, his life opened up to accommodate mine, as if such a space had been held in reserve for me. It never occurred to me at the time that that space may have had an occupant before me, and I had slipped into it like a possessionless tenant into a furnished room. He would be cooking when I came home from work. We would have a drink while I set the table and listened to the news. Before the weather changed, I built a redwook deck for the terrace of this penthouse apartment, and we ate out there till November. After dinner, he would work some more at the piano, and I did the dishes and read business magazines. Later I would join him at the piano, where we played a game we had stumbled upon by accident. Once he had been orchestrating a song for a nightclub act. The music seemed familiar to me, and after he finished the verse, I suddenly opened my mouth and essayed the chorus in my uncertain tenor. I found myself singing the lyrics to "All the Things You Are" without even knowing its title.

"How does someone your age know the words to that old song?" he asked.

"I don't know," I said. "Maybe my mother liked it."

"You have a nice voice," he said. "It's small but sweet. Like Blossom Dearie."

"Who's that?" I asked, turning away to look out the window, over the terrace, at the skyline of Manhattan.

"You're blushing," he said.

"I've never blushed in my life," I said. At that moment, everything felt exact and right and comfortable, the way you might have felt in grade school when your teacher told you to put away your books and to fold your hands on the desk because she was going to tell you a story.

"So much the better," he said. Then, turning everything into a game, he asked, "Do you know this one by Kern?" When he began the verse of yet another song, I sang the chorus.

Sometimes I watched him shave—naked and framed by the doorway and the length of the hall—in the same attitude that I might consider a painting, and I experienced that same kind of rewarding detachment. With his classical proportions, his was the kind of body that art teachers find for their students to sketch, not muscular but manly. From the bathroom, he would walk down the hall and smile at me. Space seemed sentient, and measured by the way he filled it. Watching him like this once, I knew that there was nothing more serious than the desire of one man for another, and that what we don't understand, we underestimate.

I came up behind him in the bedroom. He was examining his own body in the mirror behind the closet door. I put my hands on his waist. He looked up at me in the mirror.

"That's fat," he said. "If I didn't have it, I'd be perfect."

"If you didn't have it," I said, "you'd be my age."

He laughed abruptly at that, and as abruptly, he stopped. "You're good," he said, "very good. And you don't know how good you are."

Later that night, we were looking at pictures that he kept in a box. There was a studio portrait of a beautiful woman, his mother, and from her expression one could easily assume that she had chosen the autumnal backdrop herself from the photographer's selections. In front of it, she posed dark and dolorous, looking over her shoulder at the photographer as if to say that she had never been happy on this earth and doubted whether any of us were meant to be.

"It's such a wonderful photograph to keep in a box," I said to him. "Anyone else would have it framed and sitting on the piano."

"I've considered it," he said, "but I don't think my mother ever liked me much." Then something in his face gave way. He cocked his head away from me. His chest dropped slightly and I saw him swallow. When he looked at me again, it was as if to see how I had tricked him into saying that, and then in another moment, as if to look in a mirror to see what lines betrayed his age.

I knelt in front of him and put my head in his lap. We were both wearing bathrobes and I could feel the warmth of him against the skin of my lips.

"How I care for you," I said. This did not say what I wanted to say, but *love* was not a word we used between us. Even so, I willed some impulse in him to reach out and touch my head. This did not happen.

Then one night, he rolled away from me in bed. I could not sleep after that and went into the other room. Flipping through a guidebook to Rome, where we were to have gone together, I heard him stir in his sleep, I heard his sigh of resolution, then his bare feet on the parquet. Next, he was facing me on the couch.

"Here's a place where the Italians line up to have their shoes shined," I said. His eyebrows raised and dropped. I said, "You probably want me to move out."

He nodded. "There's no hurry," he said, smiling like a psychoanalyst.

"I could move into a hotel tomorrow."

"That wouldn't be nice for you."

"It wouldn't be for long."

"I don't want you to hate me," he said.

"If anything, I'll hate myself."

He seemed to understand that. "Will you look for an apartment in this area?"

"I know all the shopkeepers."

"Then you'll stay in the neighborhood."

"If I can find an apartment."

He considered that for a moment, was satisfied, then placed his palms on his thighs, nodded, and went back to bed.

I remained in the Mission-style rocker that he had bought for a song in graduate school, wondering whether there were such bargains still to be had, and where I might find one for myself. There were the dark-stained parquet floors, the brass pen trays, the Weller vases, the Italian sofa, the oil painting that had increased in value a hundred times since its purchase. In the hallway, there were autographs of great composers; in his bedroom, a portrait of him by a now-famous painter of the New York School. The kitchen was well shelved, well stocked, machined: copper pans, sponge-glazed bowls, Mexican tiles, bean pot, an urn of spoons and spatulas, a counter's length of cookbooks, all of it bought in the pursuit of that balance between the domestic and the sensual, and all of it a strong statement to me that I had nothing to do with the exclusive moment when any of it was purchased, the meaning it had without me, what happened before me and was happening—still. I had failed to endure, maybe not domestic, maybe not sensual enough. And even the apartment building had a history: Movies had been made here that showed up in revival houses; Stieglitz had done studies on the stairwell.

It was occurring to me, like a sensation that has not yet turned to pain, that detachment from all this would not be without its own kind of terror. I poured myself some of the expensive cognac that he had introduced me to but I had bought, and lit one of the cigars he had encouraged me to smoke. Then I sat down with his box of photographs. One of his cats jumped onto the couch and tried to climb into the box. I knocked her down somewhat too violently. She stood sideways considering my behavior, then arched her back and hissed, bolting away. I half-thought she might tell on me. The half-feral cat with the extra toes looked down on me from the bookshelf, and blinked, watching everything over the inside membrane of its eyelids.

I soon found what I was looking for: an eight-and-a-half-by-eleven glossy of him when he would have been about ten years older than I was at that very moment. He was holding a saxophone in one hand—an instrument he did not play—and a cigarette in the other, although he had never smoked. The cigarette smoke rose in a straight column in front of his black T-shirt. There was nothing on his face but a show of anger—part of the pose, I assumed—and predictions of how his face was going to age, predictions that came true. But I found myself pulled to him, drawn to him by the gravity of the photograph, the weight of its sensuality. With equal force, I felt the sheer shove of time between the moment that the photograph had been taken and the moment that I was seeing it. From that moment on, I would be looking at him from some distance, over an enormous gap that my heart leapt to cross, beat after beat, but could never, not to save my life.

I had never known this side of desire, this longing for health one recalls from childhood illnesses that modern medicine has all but eradicated, those dark miasmic fevers and the pain we asked our mothers to explain. Only out of this fever, the question is one we know better than to ask: Why can't you love me?

I put the box of photographs on the shelf where I had found it, and read a while longer, knowing that that would be an excuse to fall asleep in the chair.

Not long before I moved out, I saw him leaving our apartment building with someone closer to my age than to his. They were leaning close together, as if listening to a mutually loved passage of music.

On the mail tray inside the apartment, there was a note to me. It said that he was spending the night and the next day in Atlantic City and would I please give Gershwin, the half-feral cat, the homeopathic medicine he had himself prescribed for it.

Next to the pewter dish was a carton of slides. The date stamped on them told me that they were about five years old. Naturally, I slid the carton open and held the slides to the light. He was in a variety of standard poses in each of them, except that he was naked, and smiling as if for a passport photo that would assure the customs man, I am normal, let me into your country. This, I thought, is a man afraid of death and even more so of aging. I had to wonder: What mixture of vanity and urgency had prompted these photos? Had he shown them to anyone? Who was the photographer? Do they remain on intimate terms? Is there something I should be doing that I am not? I felt as if I was looking for clues on the white edges of these transparencies, as they are called, but there were none. I was looking for ways to reach this man and I had never been one to consider motive before.

It was very warm for May. The subways were already absorbing the heat, and the passengers looked, or did not look, at one another, as if blaming themselves for this springless year. I needed a shower before I could go out again in search of an apartment.

As I had seen him do, I watched myself in the large round ocean-liner mirror through his transparent shower curtain. An older man at my office gym had suggested that were it not for my mustache, my chest hair, I would have the body of a sixteen-year-old athlete. The man I lived with smiled at this, obviously having had the same thought himself, but suggested nothing. With his shaving brush, I lathered my entire torso, and with the straight-edge razor he taught me to use, I shaved my chest from breastbone to navel, watching the anticipated result in the huge and elegant mirror.

Looking very much indeed like a sixteen-year-old athlete, I felt a sudden tender generosity toward the world and myself, unfocused, neither self-centered nor self-exempting. Sun angled into the bathroom window and made the room and my body shimmer. I put his old silk bathrobe on. Then I went to the oversized dictionary in which I kept my father's letters.

Each had a three-cent stamp on it. I blew into the end

that my mother had torn open and shook the letter out of the envelope. With it fell a picture-booth snapshot facedown to the desk. On it was written, "Hi, honey. What do you think of me now?" I turned the picture over. There was a soldier and he had my eyes, my ears. Our cheekbones were the same height, our noses were identical, his smile was more certain but similar. The snapshot was blurry around the soldier's hat and temples, but there was fine detail and surprising depth in the open collar and the shadow on his neck.

The letter I read was written in pencil on unlined paper. I held the snapshot in one hand and read, "Honey, I look at your picture every night. Your eyes seem to dance and sparkle, and your sweet lips seem to keep saying I love you. Sweetheart, there isn't a morning that goes by that I don't think of you when I wake up. Your voice seems to go through my dreams as clear and as sweet as the stars in the sky and the sweet smell of flowers here at camp. I seem to be able to reach out and touch you, then you come to me and place your arms around my neck and I go almost wild with love for you. Darling, I lay in bed last night and thought of how we acted the last time I was with you. I can almost feel your arms around me and it makes me feel like coming to you right now. I get so involved thinking about you that the night flies by. I could never prove my love to you, honey, it's just beyond words.

"There's a beautiful moon out tonight, honey, just like the one we used to park under. It seems to look at me and smile. It says to me, Don't you worry, Joe, she's thinking of you, and she loves you as much as you love her. You'll be with her soon and speak the words of love that are being stored in your lonesome heart. Oh, darling, how can a guy like me deserve your love, you're so wonderful in every way. I love all the things you are, Lorraine. I love you more than words or actions could ever explain. My love for you will never die, Lorraine, it will never die. We'll always be together, won't we?"

* * *

The next day I went to the New York Public Library on Forty-
second Street. I didn't know what I was looking for until I
found it. On one shelf in the large reading room was a row
of telephone books for the entire country. In the books for
northwest Michigan, I found my father's address in the city
where I was born. I went back to my office and wrote him
what I thought was a wonderful letter. There was nothing
incriminating in it at all. I told him what I thought he would
want to hear: that I was a success at what I wanted to be doing,
that I expected nothing from him, and that if he didn't want
to write me back, I would understand.

The same evening when I got home, there was something
from my mother on the tray in the hall.

"Is that a birthday card?"

I looked up. He was sitting at the kitchen counter watching television while he ate. I was made hopeful on two counts:
He remembered that my birthday was at the end of the week,
and because this was the first time he had spoken to me first
in two weeks.

"No," I said to him after I'd opened the envelope. "It's
something I have to sign to make me executor of her estate
when she dies."

We both smiled at the irony of thinking it had been a
birthday card. I thought that my mouth felt like his, that my
smile had taken on the shape of his.

"That shouldn't be too much to handle," he said.

"No," I said, and managed a laugh. "It won't be at that,
although she writes that she just sold her half of the house to
my . . . to her ex-husband for fifteen thousand."

"What's she going to do with the money?"

"Buy a car, for one thing."

"That's the problem with these bourgeois," he said. "They
get a little money and they spend it."

I paused. "Did you win in Atlantic City?"

"No," he said.

There was another pause while we watched television a moment and he served himself another helping. Then I said, "I wrote my real father a letter today. I thought I'd tell you."

"Why would you do a thing like that?" he asked.

I watched the fork rise from the plate to his mouth, thankful that he was not looking at me. "You said—"

"I beg your pardon."

"You said that if I—" I tried again, but instead, "It didn't seem an inappropriate thing to do."

"You might have waited until you had a place of your own," he said. Since all my mail did come addressed to him, another man, this might have been a consideration.

"I don't suspect that it will matter in the end," I said.

"What's that?"

I signed the card that would make me executor of my mother's estate in the event of her death, and took it out in the hall to the mail chute. One moment more, my ear against the slot, I listened to the card fall sixteen floors—*foosh, foosh*, the way a doctor described the murmur of my seven-year-old heart, which would heal by itself. I recalled a conversation that I had had once with a friend when she lost her sole remaining parent.

"I've always wanted to ask," I began. "Is it at all liberating?"

She looked at me with wide astonished eyes and grabbed my wrist. "Yes," she said. "Yes."

Each time I walked into my new apartment, I had to orient myself anew, for I had a picture in my head of how it should all eventually look, and I would be slightly awed, somewhat pained to see that the wood floors had not been bleached, the harlequin pattern laid in the kitchen, the right sofa purchased, or any of the blueprints of my imagination realized yet. I was longing for things out of proportion, the way a Piranesi etching dwarfs human beings in the foreshortened area before a ruin. Yet if I longed for things with a spurious scale—one that made everything seem huge and distant in the short forefront of desire—I did not think that longing unique to me, but as common to my generation as a popular song. But to want and want and want, and not to know that you are wanting, means that you are never sure of anything. It means that you don't know how vulnerable you are, how open to attack. It means that you don't know how great the space of your longing is until there is a specific object to fill it.

The man I had lived with finally called me a month after I had moved out to tell me that Gershwin the cat had died of diabetes in an animal hospital.

He said, "I thought you would want to know since you were the only person he ever took an immediate liking to. In fact, I called to ask you to join me at the hospital, but you weren't home. The doctor had given him a two hundred-to-one chance against survival, and said that it would be less expensive to put Gershwin to sleep, but I said we had to take the chance. Cost was no consideration."

"How much did it cost?"

"Three hundred dollars. We did what we could, though." He began to cry a little into the phone. He apologized for himself and then he began to sob. I was certain that I knew what he was thinking: Had he taken the cat to the vet a month ago instead of diagnosing it himself, the cat would have lived. I suspected that if he was still crying now three days after its death, he had been blaming himself all along. I even hoped this to be the case.

"I just got back from burying him in the country where I found him ten years ago. On the way home, I wrote a eulogy for the poor thing, which I was going to deliver to you by hand. Maybe I could come over now."

I did not want him to see my apartment until it was finished. What's more, there were a couple of things I had left in his apartment in the hope that I would be able to collect them and see him again, but I never had the courage to go back uninvited. And I had also convinced myself that had he wanted to see me, he would have called. "Do I have any mail there?" I asked.

"Yes, lots," he said, more cheerful now. He began to read

me the return addresses, none of it at all important until, "And here's one from your father! Shall I bring it with me?"

"No, no," I cried out. "I'll be right there. Wait for me."

I knew I could get to him faster than he would to me, for there were twenty short blocks between us that I could run without effort. I rushed out the door without my keys, ignoring the phone as it began to ring again. A saxophone teacher who lived in my building was giving a music lesson. His student yearned to play with the urbane detachment of the teacher, but whether it was breathing, or phrasing, or whatever determines these things, I do not know; he played feelingly. And whatever his intention, it was the way he played the song that made me hear the lyrics as I ran: "Time and again I longed for adventure, something to make my heart beat the faster. What did I long for, I never, never knew."

It was that time of the year when the sun appears to set down the center of Manhattan streets. It was that hour of the evening when the dusk light makes the surface of things important. Everything seemed suddenly proportionate and complete. I felt as if I were running back in the face of time to meet a stranger to some part of myself.

The apartment door was open when I got there. I walked in and saw him sitting on the edge of the bed with the receiver of the telephone in his hand. When he smiled at me, it was with the smile of one mourner to another.

"You're out of breath," he said.

"I ran."

"You look good," he said, and embraced me. Once his face was on my shoulder, he began to cry again. He cried so hard that I had to lower him to the floor. The bottom of his sweat shirt did not cover his stomach, and I could not decide whether that was because he had put on weight or whether the shirt had always been too small for him. I sat on the edge of the bed and tried not to look at him. Something about the way he wept told me that he did not blame himself for the cat's death, after all, for having diagnosed its illness as one he suffered himself, for having prescribed it the same homeopathic medicine he had prescribed for himself. A kind of dread came over me, maybe phobic, maybe instinctual, as if I should be prepared to bolt, and which suddenly forced me to wonder, Why hadn't I ever noticed this air of failure about him before? Were all men like him? Was I?

"You have something for me?"

He reached behind him for the envelope I could see in his back pocket, and handed it to me with a grateful smile. It was the eulogy for the cat, which he then waited for me to read. His beautiful handwriting served only to make its contents that much more mawkish, made it easy to imagine him covering the Upper West Side giving individually written copies—the way music copyists write out scores—to the doormen of buildings where his friends lived, the envelopes marked BY HAND.

"I'm touched," I said. He had managed to remember me in the cat's eulogy, as if it were a will. "It's lovely." He nodded, smiled again, and looked down at the floor.

I paused with due respect. Then, "The letter from my father?"

"Oh, that," he said. He didn't move. "I tried to call you. I was only joking."

I leaned forward, as if to urge someone on in a bank line. "What's that?"

His tragic smile disappeared. "I'm sorry," he said. "I didn't think that you'd run all the way down here for that. You said he never meant anything to you." Then he smiled again.

I didn't bolt, but walking out of the apartment, I considered the value of what I was leaving behind: a Mexican knit sweater, a picture of me in the same sweater, half-obscured in shadow and dark glasses, and a hat. I went into the hall and held the call button down, hoping that the elevator man would think that there was an emergency, although the arrow above the door indicated that the opposite was true.

"I am sorry," he said from the doorway. "Really, I had

no idea. Maybe someday you'll even blame yourself," he said hopefully, meaning that someday I might forgive him.

Someday, yes, I thought, but there was no hurry. I started running down the white marble stairs. The walls were wainscoted with the same marble, although polished and not so worn, and the frosted windows made the light on the stairwell gauzy. I swung from one flight to the next around the banisters at each landing. On one of the landings below me was a model in a winter coat and a photographer with a shiny umbrella on a tripod. He had turned his camera on my descent. I could hear the accusation of his shutter release. He thought he was so lucky. But I was running too fast to stop, and I was certain that if I ran hard enough, fast enough, and in the right direction, I would find myself back in the raw heart of time, that point of detachment, and be beat out again, with nothing at all behind me.

THE
BODY AND ITS
SEASONS

=

For our own private reasons
We live in each for an hour.
Stranger, I take your body and its seasons
Aware the moon has gone a little sour
For us . . .

—THOMAS JAMES

Sara, did you come yet?" Gordon whispered.

Sara wasn't saying. Her hair was spread across her pillow like a piano shawl, and her head turned into it. The difference between sex with a man and sex with a woman, Gordon thought, was this: You knew when he was finished.

He counted on the fingers of one hand—one, two, three, four, five. Five and a half. That was the number of times he had had sex in his life. This was the fifth; the half counted for the time Father Creighton came but Gordon himself had not. Once he had had sex with two people at the same time, but he didn't know how to count that. Was that sex once, or sex twice? A woman who gave birth to twins was only pregnant once, he said to himself.

Because he had no sexual attraction for women, it never occurred to him the indifference wasn't mutual. It was Marie who told him that Sara wanted to have sex with him. Sara was his second woman. But it was Marie who had talked him into skipping Father Creighton's class, Catholic Self-Actualization: Fully Human, Fully Alive, and coming to her room for an afternoon nap. That was November, cold the very first week, an early winter.

"We'll be warmer together in my bed," Marie said. As he climbed under her blankets, he caught a glimpse out the window; it was snowing on the students who were going to class. Then she had seduced him before he even knew what was going on, before he could say that he was homosexual. And once started, it seemed embarrassing to bring up the subject.

The geography of her body was unlike anything he had ever wanted. Marie was a field of flesh, a mountainscape, when all he had ever desired was flatness and the familiar. He felt like Ruth among the alien corn. And he wondered why a woman would want to do what she was doing to him. It was clear to him why a man would do that; a man knew the effect of it, and that knowledge was part of the pleasure.

When he was in the seminary, a priest had called women the devil's gateway. Gordon thought of that in bed with Marie. He had looked down at her body beneath his with no sense of himself as sinning, of losing his tenancy in the Garden. For just what was innocence, he wanted to know? What was exactly lost when it was lost? It was a word that did not describe itself. The dictionary was no help: "free from wrong, sin, or guilt." The word shared its past with *noxious*, which meant to hurt or injure. Was he absent of harm, absent of hurt? No one seemed to have an answer.

Every night they argued the question in rehearsal for *The Garden: A Ceremony*. Rehearsals always began with group sessions, and the director wrote down what they said on a huge scroll of white paper. She was a woman named Renata. She called what she wrote down the "graffiti" of their lives. The text of the play was being developed out of their memories and confessions. He wished that he had been cast in a play where the characters spoke to one another and never said what they really meant. After six weeks of this rehearsal, he was tired of other people's sensibilities.

"When did you lose your innocence?" Renata asked. Then she looked at him because he was almost always the last to answer. He bet she thought he hadn't lost it yet.

"We come from condemned stock according to the Church," he said. "We were never innocent."

"You don't believe that, do you?" she asked.

He didn't, no. Original sin—what was the original sin? Was it simply disobedience of a domestic kind, and what had Adam and Eve been disallowed to do: eat from the tree of knowledge? And what had been the knowledge gained? Of their nakedness? Surely not so much in that, if that is indeed what they were. And the punishment: quick, put some clothes on—God made them himself out of skins, the first tailor—and get them out of the Garden before they eat from the tree of life and live eternally. The punishment: death and hard labor. And if Eve had eaten from the tree of life instead of the tree of knowledge, what would the punishment have been then, no sex?

"You don't believe in original sin," Gordon said to her, "but you do believe in an innocence that can be lost." Wasn't innocence just an old children's story that can be read with smug delight by adults, renewed over the generations by fashionably updated illustrations, more gorgeous, more expensive to reproduce? The story itself was always simple enough; it was the illustrations and elaborations that became more difficult to understand.

"Well, for our purposes, let's say that you lose your innocence after your first time."

"Then it's sex that corrupts," he said, "and not desire that comes before sex, nor even the awareness that sex is possible?"

He knew it wasn't an argument she wanted to hear, and if she wanted to hear about the night he spent with Brother Raft, what was she going to make of the fact that he had gone to Raft's room with every intention of having sex? Had he been innocent then?

Raft's room was in a new structure built far across the seminary campus, overlooking a dry ravine. It was made of cinder blocks and yellow brick. It was the winter a year before; the wind blew across the fields that surrounded the seminary; and there were no trees or bushes that could break it.

"Gordon, why are you here?" Raft had asked.

Gordon peered past the door of Raft's room. To call it a room was to exaggerate; it really was a cell, so small, so sealed off, that it smelled too much of the human who inhabited it, sour as a dirty towel. "Can I come in?" he asked.

"I could be fired," Raft said. "I could be expelled."

"I'm a minor. You could go to jail," Gordon said.

"You can stay awhile," Raft said, "but I'll warn you now. You will be ashamed of yourself in the morning."

That had not been the case. Brother Raft, his body just that for the better part of an hour, had taught him that sex was possible, and if sex was possible, then other things were as well. Gordon had been given a choice when he was fourteen years old and it was time to leave the orphanage in which he had been raised. He could join the seminary or a military academy. Since the military academy doubtlessly led to Vietnam, he had chosen the seminary. Now he realized that he didn't have to stay here, either. He began to write away for college catalogues. All the schools he applied to wanted him, especially after they had seen the Latin, all the Bible study on his transcripts. A Jesuit university offered him the largest scholarship.

"Sara," he said again, "did you come yet?"

She rubbed her head deeply into the pillow and said, "No, Gordon, no. Not yet."

What was going on down there, he wondered? Marie had been just the same, endlessly insatiable. Gordon figured that if he could have sex safely only once a month, he would be the same way himself. Marie had wanted him to come back to her room after his rehearsal that night, for it had been the last of what she called her "free days."

"How will I get in after visiting hours?"

"You'll have to stand on my shoulders and climb in through the window," Marie said.

He told her he was gay, but that didn't seem to make much difference to her. So he replied that he didn't want to climb in through the window because the Jesuits next door kept an eye on the women's dormitory for just such things.

He answered the Jesuit switchboard on weekend nights. If none of the Jesuits came down, he could study or sleep, but there was inevitably ones who came down to flirt with him, if they were sober, worse if they were drunk. The worst was Father Creighton, whose class he and Marie had skipped to have sex.

There was one textbook for Father Creighton's class. It was called *Secrets of Staying in Love*. Creighton had written it himself. It began: "Dear Brothers and Sisters of the Human Family, Perhaps you have read my other books. Forget them. They reflect where I was as a person when I wrote them. In this book I will share with you where I have come from that point, where I am now . . ."

There were no other texts or outside readings for Creighton's class. Gordon figured that Creighton feared he might pale in comparison to anything anyone else had ever written. And there were no exams. The students were graded on the degree of honesty Creighton judged in the journals he asked them to keep, their "dialogue in diary." He called dialogue the "lifeblood of love," and gave his class five hundred questions they were supposed to have answered by the end of the semester.

Creighton came down drunk to the switchboard one night. "I can usually tell how deeply a lecture has reached my students by the faraway look they get in their eyes," he said to Gordon.

"Oh," Gordon said. "Well, I suppose I get lost in thought sometimes."

"No, not you, my friend," Creighton said. "Your mind never wanders. Sometimes I feel as if you are sitting there judging me."

Gordon could tell by the slow way Creighton moved to a chair that he was a little drunk, as if the courage he needed to speak had come from the bottle. "I suspect you are the suspicious type," Creighton said. "The suspicious perceives no value in himself. And in the blind belief that everyone is really like him, he extends and projects his own self-distrust onto others."

"I can see that, Father," Gordon said.

"You probably believe that I am a megalomaniac," Creighton said, and didn't wait for an answer. He pulled his chair up closer to Gordon's. "I've read your records. You grew up in an orphanage and a seminary. No mother, no father you could call your own. That must have been painful."

Gordon said, "Yes, Father. The only time I was ever alone was when I was studying or supposed to be in prayer."

"I would like you to think of me as a parent," Creighton said. "I would like to think of you as a son I never had."

Gordon said that he was grateful, and Creighton wrapped his arms around Gordon's shoulders. Creighton began telling him a story that Gordon recognized from their textbook. It was about two brother priests who had gone through "the wearying wilderness of seminary training together. They were always there for one another, an ear, a shoulder, in time of spiritual need."

One was killed in an auto accident right outside the Jesuit community in which they lived. The other, learning that his friend was dead, rushed out and cradled the dead man's head in his arms. "You can't die," he cried out, "I never told you that I loved you."

"Was that your friend who died?" Gordon asked the priest.

"No," he said.

"You knew the other priest, then?"

"I made the whole thing up," Creighton said, standing as if to leave. "But it has an inner truth." He pulled Gordon's head against what would have been his lap if he was sitting down, and held it there. So Gordon unzipped Creighton's pants and pulled the priest out of his boxer shorts. Afterward, Creighton stumbled against the wall and made his way out of the office without even saying good night.

When Gordon got the journal back from him at the end of the semester, there was a *C* on the front page. "It was nice to learn that you are not just another pretty face," Creighton had written on it. "Come to my office if you want to talk about your grade."

Walking Sara home from the performance that night, he had told her about the grade. She had laughed. "It doesn't mean that you aren't intelligent," she said, "it just means that you're shallow."

It was one of Sara's free days. He knew because Marie had told him. Marie had become a lesbian, and Sara her only lover. Marie credited him for her sexual conversion. He wondered whether he had that effect on people.

"I just want you to know, Gordon, that this was an intellectual decision on my part," she had told him in what seemed like a prepared speech.

"Marie, I do not believe that your homosexuality is an intellectual accomplishment," Gordon said.

"It was for me. I had never given such practices any thought before I had sex with you. You made love to me and you aren't even attracted to women. And God knows if you were, I'm not the prettiest one on campus."

But he did think that she was beautiful. She had a profile like you see through the window of a jewelry store, a face on a cameo; he had seen it one day in Creighton's class. Marie had been staring out the window, probably giving the teacher the impression he had touched the deepest part of her being. Her pale blue work shirt opened nearly down to her breasts, and he could see the freckles across her white Irish skin. He'd really known so few women in his life. He looked at her. She thinks, he thought, therefore she has self-doubt. It struck him that she was fragile, though she would never think of herself as such. We were simply fragile with little choice in the matter.

Father Creighton was telling his story about the two priests. "Remember that it is your feelings that individuate you," he said. "The feelings you are having right now make you different from what you have ever been and will ever become. If you are not capable of the vulnerability required to reveal the extent of your feelings, you will never be fully human, fully alive."

Gordon wanted to say, Just look there. See that woman in the light of the window, the freckles on her breasts, the look of distraction. How could anyone be more vulnerable? Why would they want to be?

It was after that class when she told him that she had fallen in love for the first time in her life. She told him that the first time with Sara had been like the first time she went to Mass, that making love to Sara was a form of worship. But Sara had told Marie and Marie had told him that Sara was not ready to commit herself, although whether it was to being a lesbian or to being Marie's lover, Gordon was not certain.

Was Sara still sowing her wild oats with him, or was that not the right metaphor to apply to a woman?

He had come once, but Sara wasn't finished. He was numb and had to ask her whether she would mind letting him lie down for a while, and so she straddled him, and he looked up at her torso, all white and firm, so different from Marie's body, like a torso he had seen in the Art Institute, albeit about to teeter off its podium.

A man had sat on him like that once. His name was J. Eli Altgeld. Sara was looking off into space, or into the corner where the wall met the ceiling, but Jake had looked him in the eye, with his mouth wide open and smiling.

"You're watching me," Gordon had said.

"No, I'm looking at you."

"You're making me come."

"Then I'll make you come again," Altgeld said, and covered Gordon's face with one huge hand. Jake had smelled like a change of seasons, that earthy smell when the ground is changing, as in the fall after a fecund summer and the earth has spent itself, or in the spring when the earth begins to thaw, and the farmer who owned the land around the seminary would turn the soil over.

That time with Jake had been better than any other time, better than the time Gordon made love to two men at once —one black, one white—together blending like paper burning into ash in the light of the television screen, like snow falling on the black, empty cornfield beyond the cyclone fence of the seminary garden, autumn rolling over into winter.

"I've never done this before," Gordon had said.

"You mean you've never had a man inside you?" It was not what Gordon had meant, but the answer was the same. And because he was ready for it, he had not resisted when Altgeld pulled him into his lap. On the bed in front of the mirror, Gordon could watch Altgeld's mouth on his ear, one hand stroking him, the other splayed against Gordon's chest. Gordon thought it should hurt, but it didn't, not after a bit; he felt himself dissolve to the point where he was most his body and least his mind. Father Creighton wanted confession, but better than that must be this, Gordon thought, penetration.

But afterward, Altgeld had started with the questions, more intimate than Creighton's or Renata's. Questions like when did you lose your faith, and do you remember your mother, and were you ever in love with anyone? Father Creighton had said that the need for solitude was a myth. "The pockets of privacy we create as a place to run to and where no one can follow are death to the kind of human intimacy so necessary to the fullness of human life."

"I just think this intimacy thing is highly overrated," Gordon had said to Altgeld.

"You do? Why is that?" he had asked.

There was a scene in *The Garden* in which all the men in the cast, except the one who played Adam, became the serpent. "Life and death are one and the same," they said to Eve, "light and darkness, life and death, good and evil, it's all the same, and because of this, good is not good, evil is not evil, life is not life, and death is not death."

Eve ate, and a basket of apples was rolled out onto the stage. The serpent leaned into the audience and tempted them, too. Altgeld was in the audience, and stood to take an apple. Gordon had started to pull back, but the other serpents pushed him forward. Altgeld grabbed Gordon around the neck and said into his ear, "Thank you, my friend. You are beautiful."

The audience was moved, the rest of the cast almost beatific, but Gordon did not join them as they moved into the auditorium to pass out apples to the audience. He moved backstage and into the wings, and when Renata came back to see whether anything was wrong, he said, "Can't you just leave me alone?"

The cast came back; Adam and Eve were expelled from the Garden. He watched the man who played Cain to his own Abel move into position for their scene together. He was handsome in the way one thinks of animals as handsome.

The women of the chorus were saying, "God cursed the ground with thorns and thistles. In toil he meant for us to eat of it until we returned to the ground from which we came. For we are dust and to dust we shall return. The leaves will blanket us in winter, fallen fruit will sweeten our graves, and in spring the orchard's blossoms."

Our punishment for eating of the tree of knowledge was death, Gordon thought, and God had kept Abel for that purpose. Cain's sacrifice had been rejected for no apparent reason, and God had taken Abel instead. Gordon stepped back onto the stage, and into his role. He kept his eyes locked on his brother's beautiful face. We'd all be innocent, Gordon thought, if it weren't for God.

Sex was not so hard, he thought. From Marie he had learned that women could have one climax after another, and never even tell you, never let you know. He thought perhaps that Sara was not telling him something. But he didn't mind. He could feel himself coming again; it was like entering a house through a long, dark hallway. You could see a light at the end of the hall, coming through a window. And you could hear a voice saying, Come in, come, just this way, I'm back here. But there is no one. You sit awhile; you live in the house for an hour, looking at the pictures that crowd the piano top. The chairs wear skirts, and you hear music in another room, smell cinnamon in hot cider. You sit back deeply. You will stay because it's cold outside. The leaves are blowing off the trees; the ground is hard, the skeleton stalks of chrysanthemums bony with frost. The garden is empty.

PHILOSTORGY, NOW OBSCURE

=

Don't go home yet," Roxy said. "The stress will blow out whatever's left of your immune system."

"I'll have to tell my mother sometime," Preston said. "It would be cruel not to."

They were both thinking of the reception he had gotten twelve years before when he told his foster parents that he was gay. Proof that homosexuality is genetic, his foster mother had said in the chilled bland tones of her Chicago accent, since there were no homosexuals in her natural family. But Preston's foster father had been warmer. Privately, face to face, he told Preston, "We make our choices where affections are concerned," and then he touched Preston's face with an open palm, as if to show that he concealed no weapon.

Roxy remembered that night because she had come home from work and found Preston sitting in the dark, smoking cigarettes, finishing a bottle of the jug red wine that Preston called Cheap Lucy. "Are you all right?" she had asked, and he replied, "I'm all lit up with no place to shine."

Tonight, Preston Wallace was drinking sour mash, Roxy Atherton beer, Lorna Fairweather herbal tea. It was their first reunion, the three of them together at the same time, in eleven years. Other than the fact of his recent diagnosis, Preston thought that they were all taking their age wonderfully well.

Lorna said, "You don't have to tell your mother anything. You'll be the one they'll find a cure for."

"As if science were so specific or personal," he said, and smiled at the instant and dismissive optimism of Lorna's response. If he hadn't told his mother yet, it was because he expected her to mitigate his illness in the same manner. Or she would say, "Oh, didn't I read that they found a cure for that?" His father having died several years before, Preston did not anticipate the support that families give at moments like these.

Roxy asked, "Are you going onto DHPG?"

"I'm surprised you even know what it is," he said. He was even more surprised when she burst into tears.

"I've worried about you," Roxy cried, for she also knew that his medication would require a catheter inserted into a vein that fed directly into an atrium of his heart. There the drug would be diffused into his blood and sped through his body in a matter of seconds. She knew that the drug had yet to be approved by the FDA and that it was given on a compassionate-use basis. She knew, too, that nurses would teach him how to administer it to himself, so that he could do it alone, sitting at home beneath his own I.V. pole for an hour, five times a week. He would have sacks of sucrose, and a big red plastic container for medical waste. She knew as much about this disease as she could know.

Lorna began to cry as well, moved by Roxy's outburst

more than Preston's illness, for he had announced his diagnosis, cool and remote as an evening news correspondent. Lorna was taking her cue from him and he was sitting with his arms across his chest, his hands under his arms, his legs stretched out. His hair was cut in the style of someone going off to war. What had become of the vulnerable and tender man she had known? This was someone who bought whiskey in airport liquor stores, and dressed, tie, shirt, slacks, all in gray. Not even the silver hoop in his ear mitigated his Marine-like, masculine reserve.

Preston said nothing, allowing them their moment of grief, as if it was his to give, a possession he could pass on, like a keepsake. His doctor had wept giving him the diagnosis, while Preston had looked in the mirror behind the doctor's desk and the reflection seemed to tell him, "This is you now. You are a sick person. What will you think about? What will hold your interest?" He knew in the way one knew these things that his death would be a fast one, the particular infection, the harsh drug used to treat it. What is more, there was a pain under his arm that had been growing for weeks. "All I can feel is muscle," his doctor had said, patting him on the back. "I should wait for more objective evidence before digging in. Maybe you should lay off the chest exercises awhile." But they both feared lymphoma.

Preston looked around the dining room as the women wept. This had been their favorite room when the three of them lived together as undergraduates. It had a south window and the sun came in all day long. There was nothing in it but a table, chairs, and a plant, a philodendron that was in the same place he had put it twelve years ago. In the decade that the three of them have lived apart, it had grown as high as the ceiling, claiming the corner with the unfolding of each new leaf. A philodendron's name implied self-love, he thought, if one was a tree. *Philo*, love; *dendron*, tree—loving tree, or love of trees. Narcissism seemed to impel this one. Philharmonic, he thought, was love of music; philosophy, love of wisdom;

PHILOSTORGY, NOW OBSCURE / *37*

philopolemic (rare), love of war or disputes. Philter was a love potion, philander actually meant fond of men. Philostorgy, meaning natural affection, was now obscure.

"Remember the night I had food poisoning?" he asked suddenly. Lorna and Roxy looked up at him at the same time.

Lorna smiled. "We found you lying in the foyer. You were white as a ghost."

"I had to drag myself along the floor until you two could hear me call for help."

Roxy wiped her nose with a crumpled paper towel. "I'll never forget driving you to the hospital. You started hyperventilating in the car and slid under the dashboard. Then Lorna fainted in the emergency room when they put the intravenous in the back of your hand."

"I was never so sick in my life," he said and hesitated. "Until now."

Lorna said, "I remember how you wouldn't let your mother visit you in the hospital because she never visited when you were well."

Preston said, "I'd better change my standards or she'll never see me alive again." And then he laughed.

Roxy got up to tear a dead leaf from the philodendron. She dropped her head to her chest and moaned the way nails do being wrenched from wood. Lorna held her teacup against her mouth. Preston saw that it was chipped along the rim, and he wanted to tell her that bacteria lived in cracked ceramic and withstood even the heat of a dishwasher, that we are most vulnerable to things we cannot see, and that the baby she was pregnant with would not have its own immune system till it was nearly two years old, and that her own immune system was likely depressed by virtue of her pregnancy.

He said instead, "Remember when I had hepatitis?"

Though Lorna said only, "Oh, Preston," Roxy was more willing to play the straight man to this old joke of theirs. "Your hospital room was yellow," she said. "You had a yellow bathrobe, a yellow bedspread, and you were eating a banana when I came to visit. Then your doctor showed up."

Preston said, "Dr. Lo."

"Dr. Lo said that you were all yellow and you said, 'So are you.' "

Lorna laughed. "Oh, Preston, you didn't!"

"I did, didn't I, Roxy? Tell her I did."

"It was a nice color for you," Roxy said. She looked at his chest and neck. One would not guess that he was ill. His shirt stretched tightly across broad shoulders. He had joined a gym after moving to New York. The man she used to live with seemed smothered under muscle.

Preston went to the kitchen for ice. "Can I get you a beer while I'm up, Roxy?"

"Are you sure you should be drinking?" she asked.

"No, thanks for asking though," he said with his head in the refrigerator. "You've done a great job with this place. I'd like to fix up my apartment, too, but I'm only renting."

Roxy said, "I'm going to tear out your old bedroom to expand the kitchen. Which reminds me, dinner won't be ready for another half hour. Can you wait or are you dying?" She dropped her head into her hand. "Oh, Preston. I don't believe I said that."

Seeing how upset she was, he touched her face as she passed by him into the kitchen. "It's all right, my friend," he said. "It really is."

In the kitchen, Roxy opened and closed the door on the oven, the refrigerator, the cabinets. She ran hot water to feel something on her skin, and lifted the lid of the Dutch oven to have the steam from the pot-au-feu rise in her face. She toasted bread and rubbed it with garlic. She grated horseradish and blended it with crème fraîche. If anything symbolized what was different in her now than when they had lived together, it was the cooking, the need to domesticate and make her apartment into a home. For Lorna, the difference, she assumed,

were her children; for Preston, his muscular body, now perhaps, the illness. Preston had cytomegalovirus, which most
people are exposed to by the time they have reached kindergarten. It could make him go blind; it could become systemic,
but there was something Roxy was more afraid of and was
afraid to bring up—it was unlikely that a person with AIDS
would only have CMV without the presence of another opportunistic infection. Did Preston know that? she wondered.
Should she ask?

"I thought she was living with someone," Lorna whispered.

"They broke up. He wouldn't marry her. She wanted
babies," Preston said. Then they were silent again. Finally he
asked, "Are you going to have amniocentesis?"

Lorna said it wasn't necessary this time, but he wasn't
listening. In his head, he was breaking the word down: amnio,
which came from *amnion*, the membrane around the fetus, was
Greek for lamb; the cognate *centesis* meant to puncture or
perforate. When he attempted to look the word up the first
time she was pregnant, he pulled down the Oxford Bible instead of the etymological dictionary that it resembled. The
passage he opened to read: "You shall be like a watered garden.
You shall be like a spring of water, whose waters fail not."

"They did a sound scan," she said to him. "It's another
boy."

"How could they tell?"

"They saw something down there."

He smiled at her choice of words. *Down there* was where
she told the police a man had touched her, a man who had at-
tacked her one bright morning as she was getting out of her car.

"I worry about you," he said.

"Why?" she asked. "I love being pregnant." Not only
that—she had everything she had ever wanted.

"It distracts me from myself," he said.

"What about you?" she asked. "What happens next?"

"I have to wait for a room to become available at the
hospital," he said. "I don't know how much time I have,

though. I mean, I don't know how long it takes this thing to progress."

"How long will you have to have the catheter?"

"As long as I want to live," he said.

Lorna inhaled deeply through her mouth. It was as if Preston did something to the air. She had been expecting this night—and for that reason did not return his phone calls, did not write him in case he should write her back with bad news.

"What are the symptoms?" she asked now. "How does this manifest itself?"

"Bright flashes of light, a floater in my eye. It's like a dirty hair in a camera lens."

Roxy called from the kitchen, "I had one of those once. The ophthalmologist blamed it on age."

Preston said, "You must have been relieved."

Lorna felt the baby begin to stir. She rose and stood next to Preston, then placed his hands on the globe of her stomach. "Feel this," she said. He kneeled to the floor, big as Atlas holding the world, then looked up at her and smiled, saying, "He's beautiful. Name him—"

She ran her hand across his hair, which was cut so short it seemed to her touch like an animal's pelt, or upholstery on a couch. Then she backed away.

"Excuse me," she said. His old bedroom, between the dining room and the kitchen, had its own bath and she slipped into it before he could rise off the floor. The tap water was instantly cold but not cold enough to numb the sensation behind her eyes. She opened the window and scooped up a handful of snow from the sill and buried her face in it. In the mirror above the sink, she saw clots of ice melting in her hairline. She was thankful for the coming baby because people made excuses for pregnant women. Even if there were anything she could do for him, she in Chicago and he in New York, her babies would have to take precedence.

Preston had told her about this as yet unnamed disease maybe seven years before in a Chinese restaurant in New

York. "How do you know all this?" she'd asked because of his fluency in a Greek-like and latinate language of cancers, viruses, funguses, and rare pneumonias. "The gay press," he answered.

"Well," she said doubtfully.

"What do you mean, 'Well'?" he'd demanded. "Are you dismissing this?"

"Well, what do you expect me to do about it?" Her voice had tightened to match his own. "There are other concerns, you know. Look at what Reagan's doing in Central America."

"I expect you to take me seriously," he had replied. "This isn't a novelty act."

There were no towels in the unused bathroom, so she dried her face on the hem of her maternity dress and stepped into his old bedroom. Preston was standing there waiting for her. In his hand was a pale blue envelope which caught her eye instantly, for it was the kind that air mail letters are sent in. She even recognized the Italian stamps, and, of course, the handwriting was her own. Blueprints for Roxy's new kitchen and breakfast nook were tacked on the wall, but till the renovation was complete she was using the room for storage. Roxy had thrown away nothing that the three of them had shared as roommates. There was the trunk they had used as a coffee table, an end table found in the alley, a pole lamp. There was the Raggedy Ann doll the three of them had witnessed flying out of a car window and getting run over by a bus. Its face still bore the tire marks. On the wall were portraits Lorna had taken of Preston for her photography class. "Do they make you nostalgic?" she asked.

"Nostalgic? I wish she would burn all these," he said. "I don't want to be remembered like that."

He turned around and headed for the sun porch at the front of the apartment. There he pulled the letter from the envelope and read it again. As close as they had been, it was the

only letter she had ever written him. She had sent it from
Rome a year after the both of them had graduated and left
Chicago.

September
Dear Preston,

My mom just told me you called. I am so sorry not to
have been here. How much I miss you—often I can imagine you so vividly. The other day I was taking pictures of
the Tortoise Fountain and I swear I saw you walking
toward me—the sun was too strong. Thanks so much for
your letter, or rather, letters. They were a real boost to
my spirits, which at the present are, say, teetering over
the edge of that black yawning abyss. Well, that sounds
a bit too tragic.

What to say? What side of the abyss should I write from
first? Since you wrote roaring about Sean's *NYR* article
on Central America, shall I remind you that behind every
man is a woman (or another man, whatever, you're all
alike)? Yes, it was my constant reassurance, loving reassurance. Kidding aside, it is exciting, isn't it, to see him
move down from the esoteric, the nous, where no one
else lives, and to the daily world of action. He seems to
thrive, as if he has forgiven himself something, as if the
intellectual indulgence of the meaning of meaning is a
luxury most people don't enjoy (or endure), especially
people who suffer not at their own hands and minds, but
at the hands of an oppressive government.

To top it all off, Sean and I had lunch with Sartre and
de Beauvoir here in Rome!!! Just the four of us!!! We
arranged to meet at a café near the Pantheon and spent
an hour talking politics and philosophy. That is, they
talked and I listened. I think it will be one of my most
cherished memories. Perhaps one makes too much of
such people, but they are great minds and their influence

on a whole generation of Europeans and Americans is indisputable.

Engaged? No, we are not engaged. I do not know what the future holds for us. I have always felt sure about our relationship, but God, I think I deserved something easier. There have got to be simpler people in the world . . . but then they would not be Sean. He has a lovely apartment in the Campo dei Fiori and seems to know the streets like the back of his hand. Time with him is time full of itself. Writing you I realize I am contradicting the mood this letter began in. Maybe you have that effect. I sometimes take the motor bike out onto the Via Appia and buy a sandwich from one of the farm stands like we used to. Remember the roasted pig, the rosemary and garlic inside it? Once you read to me from *The Four Quartets*. You are missed now, but I know we will be together again. For the rest of our lives we will be close, it must be that way, it can be no different.

"Maybe it's time to have more pictures taken," Lorna said to his back.

She saw him put the letter in his pocket. "I've put on forty pounds of muscle weight since those pictures were taken," he said. "Maybe if I had known that that was possible back then, I wouldn't have needed the lithium."

"You don't think you need it anymore?"

"Why, am I acting funny?"

She shook her head in case he was not looking out the window but at her. "I didn't realize you had quit."

"Years ago. I think I outgrew my mood swings. Or I was misdiagnosed in the first place. Maybe they just seemed the norm in New York. A friend once told me that I was always depressed, and I said to him, no, actually, that I was profoundly happy. But that never struck me as true until I said it."

A therapist had once told Preston that depression was likely to be his natural state, where the gravity of his mind would keep him despite all attempts at levity; but now it seemed that even when he was depressed there was a tow rope of some kind dragging him back toward happiness.

"I've never heard you say it either," she said, for having heard it from his lips she also believed it. "Are you seeing anyone now?"

"A man?"

"No, a therapist."

"Talking about this won't make it go away," he said.

He could sense her trying to think of something to say. Her discomfort was comforting. It was proof to him that she recognized the end of the friendship as described in her letter, and that she was responsible for it. He had intended to give her the letter as a souvenir of their friendship, and now he realized that doing so would be like an indictment.

"An article I submitted about grief in the gay community was rejected by *The Journal of Sociology*," he said. "The peer-review panel didn't believe that gay men could suffer bereavement. They said our relationships were too shallow."

"Was that the only reason they gave?" She saw him stiffen at that, and amended it to, "Surely that's not the reason they gave for rejecting you."

"I got a phone call last week from a woman who asked me if I was a friend of her brother, Fred Pais," he said. "I said yes, and she said, 'I'm sorry to tell you this, but he's passed away.' She was calling everybody in his address book, which is what I always imagined you doing for me. Since my address book was filled with names of the dead because I couldn't bring myself to remove them, one for practically every letter of the alphabet, I thought I should start a new one, for your sake. It's tighter than the old book but lacks the emotional resonance, if you know what I mean."

Lorna said, "It hasn't touched our lives the way it has yours."

"You have an inquisitive mind," he said.

"The baby takes up so much time."

"You don't even return my phone calls," he said. "I talk to Sean every time I call. I didn't even know you were pregnant again until you walked through the door; you didn't call me when the last one was born. You knew I was sero-positive. How much time did you think I had?"

"We never thought it would go this far."

"But it's always been there, Lorna," he said. "You knew people were dying. Didn't you ever even think that I might know some of them?"

"You're right, Preston," she said. "I'm sorry."

"I always thought that you would be there for me."

"I will now."

"You're going to have another baby in three months. By the time you've weaned it, I could be dead."

She started sobbing at that. "Tell me what I can do for you."

"I could send you a pamphlet called *When Someone You Know Has AIDS*. It's filled with helpful hints for friends of the afflicted," he said. "Or, better still, you could continue on as if I never existed."

That gave her an exit. She pushed her arms into the sleeves of her coat as if it were a life jacket and was out the door. That was what she must have wanted, he thought, an annulment. When Lorna had entered the apartment that night, she immediately said that she could not stay. "Take your coat off," he had told her, "this will take more than fifteen minutes." That's when he saw that she was pregnant again. He listened to her running down the steps, and from the sun porch he could see her walking briskly up Sheridan Road. It was below freezing, but he suspected that the cold night air felt good against her face.

After the doctor had given him his diagnosis, Preston had gone home and begun to clean his apartment. He took blinds from the windows and soaked them in the tub. He took books from their shelves and wiped them with a damp rag. He polished brass and waxed wood and relined shelves with new paper till the apartment was astringent with the smell of powder cleanser and bleach. The cleaning was an addictive tonic that kept him going for three days.

Not satisfied with surfaces, he emptied the closets of clothes that didn't fit anymore or had gone out of style (kept out of a lower middle-class phobia of waste). He threw out gifts he never wore, and impulse purchases that proved his taste was not impeccable. Bureau drawers gave up a T-shirt proclaiming SO MANY MEN, SO LITTLE TIME, old jock straps, unmatched socks, silk shirts and silk underwear he wouldn't be caught dead in. He had once read an article by a journalist whose neighbor had died of AIDS. The writer had described the contents of the dead man's garbage, reducing an entire life to a leather vest, chaps, and sex toys. Writing about the clothes was more invasive than wearing them would have been, he thought. And he thought about what people would find cleaning out his own apartment.

Into the night, Preston threw out record albums and photograph albums, school diplomas, high-school literary magazines, ribbons won at speech tournaments, his draft card. Did he cling to this stuff or did it cling to him? he wondered. How much space should the past be given in a one-bedroom apartment? The police showed up because the neighbors were worried, and Preston asked them when it was legal to throw away old tax returns. (He threw the recent ones away as well. What could they do to him now?)

Only his college notebooks slowed the process down, as if there should be a reason to stave off their destruction, as if there was something in them he might have forgotten and needed learning again. He found notebooks for classes he couldn't remember having taken, he read half sentences followed by exclamation points, dates that were starred and circled; he had to wonder what fault, or lack, or need, or uncertain sentience had responded to the teachers' lectures with such useless scribbles. Better to throw it all away than to have someone find it, lay claim to it, or reduce his life to it.

Worse were the journals. Inside these were drafts of poems
he had tried to write when he was still in college: "The Moth
and the Flame" ("This is the darkness, this is the light / I cannot
make it more simple than that"); "The Gas Chamber" ("Its
lips are as tight as a bronze virgin"); "The Dark Horse" ("The
dark horse died today. It should have been expected"); then
"Stillborn," "Allergy," and "Freesia." Preston ripped the pages
from their black bindings, then burned them in the sink like
love letters after a divorce till there was nothing left but ash
and smoke that hovered near the ceiling and made the fire
alarm scream like a banshee. He needed to do the same with
old friends, affect their memory of him, introduce himself anew
and say, "This is me now."

Some things he saved: letters from friends, and two papers
he had written in college, one on the Pardoner from *The Can-
terbury Tales,* and one on Walt Whitman. "The first angry
homosexual," he had written about the Pardoner, "the first
camp sensibility in English literature." And then there was
Whitman's vision of love between two men, almost a civic
duty, and one that had flourished for a while. The latter paper
he had turned in late with a note to the teacher, "I have gotten
a disease in a Whitmanesque fashion, perhaps a hazard from
the kind of research I have been doing lately." Something had
made the glands in his legs swell up till it was impossible to
walk. "Are you homosexual?" the school doctor asked, having
seen the same infection in the gay neighborhood where his
practice was. "Well, now that you mention it," Preston replied.

"Dinner will be ready soon. I need your help in the
kitchen," Roxy said to his back. "What were you thinking
about just now?"

"Sexually transmitted diseases."

"Well, be sure to wash your hands," she said.

"I had so many of them back then I should have gotten
an honorary degree in public health," he said. "You connect
that with this, don't you?"

"It's hard not to," she said.

"I used to pray that you would be asleep when I brought

men home," he said. "Otherwise, you would turn the charm on and I would never get them to bed."

"I suspect that's what I had in mind as well," although she did not tell him that it seemed as if she stopped existing when he brought strangers back from the bar where he used to work. "I'm Roxy," she would tell them. "I was named after the movie theater in which I was conceived. Someone had turned on the cloud machine and there were stars in the ceiling. My mother was only worried about how she would preserve her wrist corsage."

Now she thought of a list of things that could kill him: *Pneumocystis carinii* pneumonia, Kaposi's sarcoma, lymphoma, toxoplasmosis, cryptosporidiosis, mycobacterium tuberculosis, cytomegalovirus, Hodgkin's disease, multifocal leukoenceph-alopathy, encephalitis, cryptococcal meningitis—over twenty-five diseases that constituted a diagnosis of AIDS. She thought of wasting-away syndrome and dementia. On her nightstand and desk was a pile of books on the immune system, subscriptions to treatment updates, newsletters out of San Francisco and New York. She knew as much about the subject as anyone could. And she thought of the Frank Lloyd Wright up the street that Preston had admired; in 1978, the year he moved to New York, it could have been bought for a hundred thousand dollars. There were things, that when you bought them, made you feel immortal.

Roxy looked around the room. "Where's Lorna?"

"She left rather suddenly. Something I said."

"Oh, Preston. I hardly ever get to see her anymore. You know how married people are," she said.

Preston loved the illicit smell of steam rooms, the way he loved the smell of cigars, or the whiskey-soaked wood of old bars. Sean wore a towel around his waist, though the steam enveloped him like a screen; Preston did not wear one, though he knew he should be concerned about the fungus and herpes that thrived in the heat, the dark, the puddles of sweat on the ceramic. Sean, Preston suspected, had brought him into the faculty steam room either to drive the despicable Jesuits out of it, or because of the way Preston eyed the students, homogeneous in their haircuts and their tangible innocence, in their Spandex shorts and bicycle pants that held their genitals up high as forbidden fruit, heavy as a Tre Scalini truffle between their legs. But he had also watched them stash their notebooks in their lockers, and wondered how much of their education would be of use to them.

Preston said, "The pilot forgot to turn off the P.A. system after he told us that we had reached cruising altitude, so the whole plane heard him when he told the copilot, 'I could sure go for a cup of coffee and a blowjob right now.' The stewardess started running up the aisle, and the man sitting next to me shouted, 'Don't forget the cup of coffee!' "

Preston could smell Sean, a rich, bitter, earthy smell, like sculptor's clay. He ran his hand across his chest and under his arm. There was a gland swollen in his arm the size of a golf ball.

"You look really good," Sean said.

"I doubt I'll be able to keep this up once they put the catheter in," Preston said.

"Where will it go?"

"Right here," Preston said, and pushed his finger against his heart where the blood that drained beneath the pressure left a white print. "I was cleaning out closets the other day, and found my notebooks from your classes."

Sean said, "I have a nightmare that everything I have ever tried to communicate will only be remembered through my students' notebooks."

"Don't worry, I threw all mine away," Preston said. "I suspected you were educating me beyond my intelligence."

"You were one of my most sensitive students."

"You mean, I saw things feelingly."

"You can't discount what you learned," Sean said, although he could not argue Preston's assessment of himself as a student. Preston had been a student who took things to heart instead of learning them. It was for students like him that Sean had inverted Socrates' "An unexamined life is not worth living" into "An unlived life is not worth examining."

Sean had been one of those students himself. Eighteen years old, he had bawled like a baby while reading St. Augustine's *Confessions* in the bathtub. The book wet in his hand, tears streaming down his face, he had taken Augustine's prayer as his own: "Whisper in my heart. Tell me you are there." There was nothing wrong with learning like that, he thought, it had a tendency to stick.

Preston never felt that Sean had thought much of his intelligence. When Preston had requested a letter of recommendation to graduate school, Sean had written, "For Preston Wallace, style is sacrament—an outward sign of inner grace." It was a personal compliment that Preston cherished, but it didn't say whether or not he could do the work.

Preston said, "Do you remember, you called your intro class 'The Crisis of Meaning.' There was the Religious Crisis, the Psychoanalytic Crisis, and the Existential Crisis."

"And I probably dragged you through all three of them," Sean said.

"I sometimes wondered if you knew what you were doing."

"I probably didn't."

Preston leaned forward into the steam to see Sean's expression. He doubted his sexuality made Sean nervous, but he was not sure. "You used to move about the classroom like a half-feral priest," he said. "I'll never forget when you opened your copy of *The Confessions*. It opened in the palm of your hand to 'We had forgotten what we had left behind and were intent on what lay before us.'"

"Something remains," Sean said, "Augustine and his mother at Ostia. You have a good memory."

"I've been refreshing it." Preston recited from recent memory, " 'The flame of love burned stronger in us and raised us towards the eternal. At last we came to our own souls and passed beyond them. And while we spoke of the eternal, longing for it and straining for it with all the strength of our hearts, for one brief fleeting instant we reached out and touched it. Then with a sigh, we returned to the sound of our own speech, in which each word has a beginning and ending.' And you stood there in your dirty blue jeans with tears in your eyes, and you sighed into the book as if love had been the lesson for the day. No wonder Lorna and I had such a crush on you."

"Blame it on my youth." Sean smiled with what Preston called "that bandaged look" straight men get in the presence of a homosexual. But Sean was thinking of another passage from Augustine: "Tears alone were sweet to me, for in my heart they had taken the place of my friend."

Preston pressed on. "There was a lecture titled 'The Death Instinct.' You asked, 'How can we unrepress Eros and Thanatos and put them into a unity that would be the basis for humanity?' "

"Well, Freud did."

"I wish I could take your class again. I think I would find it more entertaining."

"It's not the mannered soap opera you seem to remember. The course is more political now. I've even taken students to Nicaragua."

"I'm surprised you have to go so far from home," Preston said.

Sean paused for a moment. He said, "Lorna came home very upset last night."

"You think I'm to blame?"

"I imagined it might have to do with your illness."

" 'Tears alone were sweet to me,' " Preston said. "Do you know she once accused me of being jealous of her for getting you?"

"I thought you were jealous of me," Sean said. "Do you remember that night in Rome when we first went out to dinner? We ate in a beer hall."

Preston said, "Walking by the Il Gesu you sang 'Recondita Armonia.' A policeman asked you to be quiet and praised your voice at the same time."

"And you kept walking between me and Lorna," Sean said. "I thought you were trying to keep us apart."

"I just didn't want to be excluded," Preston said.

Memory, Preston had always thought, was like an old bomb shelter, holding cans of Del Monte, boxes of Bisquick, forgotten gifts of expensive wine. He had begun to learn, however, that the body can recall things on its own. There were nights when he felt the recent dead getting into bed, climbing over him as if they had just come from the shower. He felt their bodies against his own, or beneath him, a sack of balls loose between their legs, wet hair on the nape of their necks. He could feel the way each of them used to push into the mattress on their way to sleep. It was even comforting to have them there, to be remembered by them before they got up to lie briefly, like this, in someone else's bed. There were dead men he could still arouse himself for.

From his pocket he pulled out another letter he had saved. "Preston, dear Preston," he read.

> Just got your letter, and am glad that you're OK. I don't understand the depths your depressions reach at these times, and wonder if they aren't somehow preventable on your part. It sounds as if that is the effort you are now trying to make. I am glad you joined a gym. I find it helps me a lot.
>
> A couple of things I have figured out: I don't want to get married or have kids, live in the suburbs, or duplicate my parents' lives, although they are happy. You were and are the closest thing, person, that is, to the dream I had of what I want, and so I was scared of you. I didn't expect you quite so soon, didn't think you'd come so easy. Being with you, seeing you, acknowledging that you actually existed, confronted me with someone that I didn't want

to know could really exist. When I am able to deal with my homosexuality—and despite what we've done together in bed and the bars we've been to together and the clap I gave you, this is the first time I have used that word to describe myself—I will be better able to be with you. Up to you, and now, I have not met anyone that I am attracted to who has a mind I can deal with. You scare me a bit.

Write, love, Jim

There were times when things, like love or a pact with life, seemed possible only in the past. It was finding Jim's letter that made Preston finally realize what Eliot had meant by mixing memory and desire, a combination so intoxicating, Preston feared the room would begin to spin, that he might need help out of his clothes and into bed, and his head held if he was to sleep. The letter went right to his head and set off a chain of events that had never even happened. In his mind, in the past, love had proved itself on a daily basis. He did not think it would ever be possible in real time again.

That was his one regret, not that many options were closing off to him, just that one. It wasn't reasonable to believe that he could arouse old feelings in Jim Stoller, but he also believed that one has to ration reason. Preston believed that he would survive, not the illness, but death itself. It was one of those things that one believes despite one's self, a tiny bubble of thought that hangs suspended somewhere between the heart and mind, fragile and thin as a Christmas tree ornament yet managing to last decades. He believed in his consciousness, that it would do more than last, but would have impact and consequence, that wherever it went, there would be discourse and agitation; decisions would be made and adhered to.

Preston tried Jim Stoller's old home number, but it was no longer in service. He dialed the number on a ten-year-old business card Jim had sent with the letter, but the receptionist at the architectural firm did not know him.

Preston said, "I'm the executor of the estate of a friend

of Mr. Stoller's. I have something to give him his friend wanted him to have." And then he tossed the ball in her court. He said, "You really must help me. I don't know how else to reach Mr. Stoller." He bargained on the lie, that the community of gay architects in Chicago would be so small that someone in that office would know Jim's whereabouts. Of course, he didn't even know for certain whether Jim was still alive. The receptionist said that she would ask around and call him back in half an hour.

He wandered into Roxy's bedroom. She once had snapshots of her ex-lover—who had posed for her naked, on a dare, on a golf course—stuck in her bureau mirror. The man had had a beautiful body. And Roxy loved telling Preston about him. Paul once had said to her, "Roxy, I want you to come as hard and fast as a freight train." And she replied, "But freight trains come real slow." "Oh, wrong metaphor," he said.

Beneath the phone on her nightstand he saw a photocopy of an article from *The New England Journal of Medicine*. It was on an experimental drug for which protocols were just being established in Manhattan. His first thought was that by the time the drug could be proved effective, it would be too late for him. Beneath that article he found treatment updates out of San Francisco, which Roxy would have had to subscribe to in order to get. As he looked through the papers on her desk, he found descriptions of other drug protocols at Chicago-area hospitals, pamphlets about herbs and the miracles expected from them, a book on the immune system and one published by the National Academy of Science, and a list of gay doctors.

Once her mother, who did not know he was gay, said to Roxy, "You know what Preston needs? He needs a girlfriend. Oh, not for sex, but just someone he can sit and talk and have a beer with." And Roxy had cried out, "What do you think I'm here for?" And more recently, a joke he made about how easy it would be to find a woman to marry was met with a long silence on her end of the line. Finally, she said, "I'd kill you."

He thought about Roxy's wrist the night before, a kind of watch on it that he did not think women wore anymore. Tears had slid down her wrist and off her watch, and now they seemed to tear across the darkness, the way the headlights of a passing car can illuminate rain as it courses down a window. He thought back and saw that a tossed-off joke, a moment of hilarity, could cover a deep resentment, that a Xerox from a medical journal could be like a love letter never sent.

When the phone rang, he realized that he had not breathed deeply in several minutes. He had a habit of holding his breath, he held it when he combed his hair, at the gym his trainer admonished him, "Breathe, Preston." At night, he woke himself out of a deep sleep gasping for air, once three times within an hour.

The receptionist called him back with the firm where Stoller was working. Preston called there, but Stoller was in a meeting and wouldn't be out for forty minutes. Instead of leaving a message, Preston began to dress to meet Stoller. He put on a deep green shirt and a plum-colored tie, which brought out the flecks of color in his tweed jacket. His trousers were rust, his cowboy boots added an inch of height. He caught a taxicab and was sitting in the reception area of Stoller's office as the architect was walking his clients to the door.

"Jim," Preston whispered when the elevator door closed on the clients.

Stoller stared through an overlay of memory. "My God," he said when he recognized Preston, "I thought you were dead."

"Well, I suppose we'll all be someday," Preston said. Stoller reached down and lifted him from the deep seat of the Le Corbusier chair. They embraced like jocks, like athletes after a winning game.

"You look terrific. If you'd looked this good ten years ago, I wouldn't have let you move to New York," Jim said. "What are you doing here? Tell me you just bought a brownstone and need an architect."

"I just wanted to see you," Preston said.

"What are you doing now?"

"I work in the Department of Thanatology at Columbia. I'm doing a study there, on bereavement in the gay community."

Stoller paused. "No, I mean *now*. We can have lunch. There's a restaurant up the street this firm restored. I live upstairs from it. You can come up and see my place."

In the restaurant, their drink orders taken, Jim pointed out the details of the room. He had headed the research team that recovered the light fixtures from the archives of a famous Chicago architect, the patterns for the upholstery and wallpaper from New York's Cooper-Hewitt Museum; the missing table sconces, the salt and pepper shakers, and the flatware had taken weeks of detective work. He said that tracing down the lost designs was like finding the original meaning of a word in a dictionary. "Do you still look up words like that?" Jim asked.

"Sometimes, despite myself," Preston said. "You used to say that when you grew up you wanted to be visionary."

"Well, I'm heavily into restoration now." Jim smiled.

Preston asked about Jim's lover. "I can't remember his name . . . Was it Seth?"

"Enoch."

"Right. Who ascended straight to heaven."

"I don't think so. But we're still together."

"You make that sound tentative," Preston said.

"We're afraid of splitting up. We're afraid of trying to start all over with someone new. There's so much you have to know about someone nowadays before you start a relationship, isn't there? Sometimes I'm glad you didn't persuade me to move to New York."

"What do you mean?" To hide the trembling of his hands, Preston buttered a breadstick and rolled it in the architecturally significant cheese bowl.

Jim said, "There's more of it there."

"It's here, too, as I recall."

"Not in the magnitude."

Preston asked, "Have you both been tested?"

"No, neither of us think we could manage knowing that we were sero-positive," Jim said.

"I've heard that one before. People are capable of living with more knowledge than they allow themselves, I think," Preston said. "Of course, there are all kinds of denial."

"What about you?"

"I have it."

"You're positive?"

Preston said, "More than positive. I was just diagnosed."

Jim's lips parted slightly. He stared for a moment, made a tent of his hands, and hid his face under it. "I can't believe how stupid I just was."

Preston said, "I should have told you we'd be playing hardball."

"I'm sorry, Preston. I guess I've been one of the lucky ones. I haven't lost anyone who was close. You used to say that architects were all whores, but it's not really true."

"You must really be glad you didn't move to New York now," Preston said. He opened his leather portfolio and pulled out Jim's letter. "Do you remember this? It's ten years old."

Jim smiled uncertainly at the self-conscious, architectural handwriting of his youth. As he read the letter, Preston said, "You know, I still remember the night we met. You were wearing a tan corduroy jacket with patches on the elbows, a blue shirt, and a rep tie undone at the collar. You ordered a Heineken. I remember your face in the light of the pinball machine, the fact that your hair was thinner than mine, and the way you smiled when I asked if I could join you."

Jim smiled again, despite the sudden, knotted sadness in his throat. Preston said, "I may live to regret saying this, but then again I might not: There is no one, no one anywhere in the world, and I've been around, whose mouth I remember like I remember yours. You still have the same shit-eating grin, and you still use it to great effect."

"I know that."

"I can remember your skin. It was powdery, like a boy's. In bright light your eyes were the color of green beach glass . . . Of course, you were wearing contact lenses, but so what? You weren't the first, and by God, I could probably figure that there were hundreds after you, but when I think of them all—and I've had to for studies because they all want to know how many men you've been with—I always think of you. I don't have any regrets, but sometimes I wonder if you had come to New York when I asked you to, if things would be different now. You could call that examining the unlived life, but the imagination knows what it will know. I can recall you coming home from work at night with irises. You've had a bad day. I get you drunk on cognac so you would be more pliable in bed. I can recall holding you when you were grumpy and stale and loose-limbed with a fever, and even how happy you were when your bowling team won. The last ten years would have been nice with you, I think. That is not to say that I blame you for anything. In any case, I brought you something."

Preston handed a square box over to Jim, who opened it as if there was risk involved. Inside was a bowl of hand-carved, sandblasted glass, just larger than a softball. In its surface were philodendron leaves, carved against deep green glass. The jagged edges of the bowl's mouth were the split leaves.

"I don't know what to say," Jim said. "It's the most beautiful thing anyone has ever given me."

"It's signed on the bottom. It was incredibly expensive," Preston said. "I wanted to make sure you got it. You were the only person I knew who would appreciate it. I've been giving lots of things away: vases, polished shells, etchings."

"You talk—I mean, you're acting as if you're giving in to this thing. They might find a cure; you could live for years," Jim said and began to cry. A waiter came to the table and walked discreetly away.

"I thought of it as clearing space," Preston said, "my own form of denial."

"I'm overwhelmed," Jim said.

"I am not without my own designs."

Jim excused himself. Preston was so pleased with the effect that he had had on Jim that his excitement sharpened the blurred edges the drink had given him. While Jim was away, he ordered another. For a moment he considered writing Jim a note and leaving. He even called the waiter back to ask for the check. The waiter, however, told him that the check had already been paid, and Preston panicked at the thought that Jim had indeed left him. But then he saw him coming out of the telephone booth.

Jim said, "I had to call Enoch about tonight. We're meeting at Orchestra Hall. You and I used to get student passes, remember? Enoch and I've had a subscription for years, but I always think of you when we get there, something about the slope of the aisle. He's always been jealous of you for being my first."

"I never knew I was."

Jim said, "We live in this building," as if it was a fact that might be disputed. "Would you like to come up?"

"Don't you have to be back at your office?" Preston asked.

"I also called them to say I wasn't coming back today."

"What was your excuse?"

"That I was spending the afternoon with a friend who just found out he has AIDS," Jim said. "Come on, we don't have much time." He reached across the table and gently tugged on the sleeve of Preston's shirt, pulling a quarter inch of cuff beyond the sleeve of his jacket.

"It's too dangerous," Preston said.

"I'm not afraid of you anymore," Jim said. "And I want some say in how you remember me."

The cold night air felt like cocaine in his nostrils. Preston had the doorman get him a taxi, hoping to get on the Drive before rush hour began and home before Roxy got off work. It was not as dark outside as it appeared from the east-facing windows of Jim's apartment. Intersections and ramps were beginning to thicken and clot with cars and buses, and though it was mostly behind him, he felt the surge of human traffic pushing him forward, like Jim's hand between his shoulder blades, and then later, Jim inside him, which was not something he had expected ever to feel again. The smell of Jim was still on his beard, the taste of him under his tongue. If he had been Jim's first lover, he suspected that Jim would be his last. "Dear Jim," he wrote in a note left on the nightstand, "I have set the alarm so that you will wake in time to get to Orchestra Hall. I suspect and hope that somewhere I stalk your dream, that you'll wake from it, and find that I'm not here, and attempt to go back to it. I'm in the book. Please call me."

Roxy was waiting for him. She left work early but still had the blush of cold on her face. She was standing on the sun porch, looking down on the traffic. "Lorna's coming in a few minutes. She wants to take you for a drive."

She pointed to the wall where the tenants previous to them—Japanese students at the Art Institute—had carved something in the plaster. "Do you remember this? I wonder what it means." She asked, "Do you still have that beautiful platter they left?" Both of them had wanted it, but she had let him take it to New York because she thought he had appreciated it more.

"Yes," he said, "would you like it back?"

"It depends on the cost," she answered.

"It will be cheaper if I send it to you now."

"Would you consider moving back here? There's plenty of room. You could be close to your family without having to live with them."

"I have a good doctor in New York. I trust him," he said. "But I'll think about it."

She asked him whether it wasn't the case that people with CMV usually had other opportunistic infections. "Nothing yet," he said, holding back the pain under his arm.

Instead, he said, "I'm sorry things didn't work out for you with Paul. He sounded good for you. He made you laugh. He made you exercise. He got you to quit smoking."

"Actually, he used to kick cigarettes out of my hand," Roxy said. "And when I got up at six in the morning to go to the gym before work, he told me to wear sweat pants because tights made my ass look like a tea bag."

"I thought you tossed him out because he wouldn't marry you."

Roxy said, "I got pregnant. He told me that it was fine with him if I kept the baby, but that he wouldn't be tied down. When I had an abortion, he was furious. He said I should have known that he wanted it. He said that I should have known what he was really feeling. That's when I told him to move out. After I had aborted my baby."

Preston hesitated a moment, then said, "You'll find someone else, Roxy. You're beautiful, intelligent. Great sense of humor."

"Oh, Preston. I'm so common I could be a franchise." She pulled a letter from her jeans pocket. "I saved this letter that you wrote me after you moved to New York. 'Dear Roxy,' " she read. " 'Right before I was to leave for the airport, I looked out the sun-porch window, and saw you standing across the street on the corner of Sheridan Road. You were wearing your jeans and green silk shirt, the tail of which was pulled out of your pants. Your hair was blowing behind you in the wind off the lake, and your blouse clung to your breasts. You had gone across the street to buy cigarettes, which were in your hand. You were watching the light, waiting for it to change, and I was watching you, wishing that it never would.' "

He looked down in the street where she would have been standing ten years before. Lorna was standing on that corner now. The wind whipped her hair under her chin and up the other side of her face. She was waiting for the light. Automatically, a habit from the days they all had lived here, she looked up at the sun-porch windows to see who was home.

Preston said, "Then my wish came true."

THE
TIMES AS
IT KNOWS US

=

Time will say nothing but I told you so,
Time only knows the price we have to pay.

—W. H. AUDEN

With regard to human affairs," Spinoza said, "not to laugh, not to cry, not to become indignant, but to understand." It's what my lover, Samuel, used to repeat to me when I was raging at the inexplicable behavior of friends or at something I had read in the newspaper. I often intend to look the quote up myself, but that would entail leafing through Samuel's books, deciphering the margin notes, following underlined passages back to where his thoughts were formed, a past closed off to me.

"Not to laugh, not to cry, not to become indignant, but to understand," he would say. But I can't understand, I'd cry, like a child at the end of a diving board afraid to jump into the deep end of the pool.

"Then let go of it," he would say. "I can't," I'd say about whatever had my heart and mind in an insensible knot. And he would come up behind me and put his arms around me. "Close your eyes," he'd say. "Close them tight. Real tight. Tighter."

Samuel would tell me to reach out my arms and clench my fists. "Squeeze as hard as you can," he would say, and I would, knowing that he believed in the physical containment of emotions in a body's gesture. "Now, let go," he would say, and I did. If I felt better, though, it was because his mustache was against the back of my neck, and I knew full well that when I turned my head, his mouth would be there to meet mine.

The day that Samuel went into the emergency room, he took a pile of college catalogues with him, not suspecting this hospital was the only thing he would ever be admitted to again. I got to him just as a nurse was hanging a garnet-colored sack above his bed. Soon a chorus of red angels would be singing in his veins. He told me he wanted to go back to school to get a degree in Biomedical Ethics, the battlefront he believed least guarded by those most affected by Acquired Immune Deficiency Syndrome. "Do you think you'll need an advanced degree?" I asked. His eyes opened, and his head jerked, as if the fresh blood had given him new insight, anagnorisis from a needle.

"That's not what I meant to say," I said. He said, "Not to worry." He died before they knew what to treat him for, what an autopsy alone would tell them, before he could even be diagnosed.

Vergil said, "Perhaps someday even this stress will be a joy to recall." I'm still waiting.

PART I

Noah called Perry a "fat, manipulative sow who doesn't hear anything he doesn't want to hear."

The endearments "fat" and "sow" meant that the argument we were having over brunch was still on friendly terms, but "manipulative" cued us all to get our weapons out and to take aim. Perry was an easy target, and we had been stockpiling ammunition since Tuesday, when an article on how AIDS had affected life in the Pines featured the seven members of our summer house. Perry had been the reporter's source. It was Saturday.

"What I resent," Joe said, newspaper in hand, "is when she writes, 'They arrive at the house on Friday night to escape the city. When everyone is gathered, the bad news is shared: A friend died that morning. They are silent while a weekend guest, a man with AIDS, weeps for a few moments. But grief does not stop the party. Dinner that night is fettucine in a pesto and cream-cheese sauce, grilled salmon, and a salad created at one of New York's finest restaurants.' "

Perry said, "That's exactly what happened that night."

"You made it sound as if we were hanging streamers and getting into party dresses," said Enzo, who had cooked that meal. "It was dinner, not the Dance of the Red Masque." He put a plate of buttered English muffins in front of us, and four jars of jam from the gourmet shop he owned in Chelsea.

Joe said, "I don't like the way she implies that death has become so mundane for us, we don't feel it anymore: Paul died today. Oh, that's too bad; what's for dinner? Why couldn't you tell her that we're learning to accommodate grief. By the way, Enzo, what's the black stuff on the pasta?"

"Domestic truffles. They're from Texas," he answered from the kitchen counter, where he was mixing blueberries, nectarines, apricots, and melon into a salad.

Stark entered the fight wearing nothing but the Saks Fifth Avenue boxer shorts in which he had slept. "Just because our lives overlap on the weekend, Perry, doesn't give you rights to the intimate details of our health." His large thumb flicked a glob of butter and marmalade off the front of his shorts and into his mouth. Our eyes met. He smiled, and I looked away.

"What intimate details?"

Stark took the paper from Joe and read aloud, " 'The house is well accustomed to the epidemic. Last year, one member died, another's lover died over the winter. This year, one has AIDS, one has ARC, and three others have tested positive for antibodies to the AIDS virus.' "

"She doesn't identify anybody," Perry protested.

"The article is about us, even if our names are not used," Enzo said. He placed a cake ring on the coffee table. Noah, who had just had liposuction surgery done on his abdomen, looked at it nostalgically.

Perry, on the other hand, was eating defensively, the way some people drive a car. "I was told this was going to be a human-interest piece," he said. "They wanted to know how AIDS is impacting on our lives—"

"Please don't use *impact* as a verb."

"—and I thought we were the best house on the Island to illustrate how the crisis had turned into a lifestyle. But none of you wanted your name in the paper."

I said, "How we represent ourselves is never the way the *Times* does."

"They officially started using the word *gay* in that article," Perry said, pointing to the paper like a tour guide to the sight of a famous battle.

"It didn't cost them anything," I said. Indeed, the *Times* had just started using the word *gay* instead of the more clinical *homosexual,* a semantic leap that coincided with the adoption of Ms. instead of Miss, and of publishing photographs of both the bride and the groom in Sunday's wedding announcements. And in the obituaries, they had finally agreed to mention a gay man's lover as one of his survivors.

"You're mad at me because she didn't write what you wouldn't tell her," Perry said to me.

Noah said, "We are mad at you because we didn't want to be in the piece and we are. And you made us look like a bunch of shallow faggots."

"Me?" Perry screamed. "I didn't write it."

Noah slapped the coffee table. "Yes, you, the media queen. You set up the interview because you wanted your name in the paper. If it weren't for AIDS, you'd still be doing recreation therapy at Bellevue."

"And you'd still be stealing Percodan and Demerol from the nurses' station."

"Yeah," Noah shouted, "you may have left the theater but you turned AIDS into a one-man show. The more people die, the brighter your spotlight gets."

"I have done nothing I am ashamed of," Perry said. "And you are going to be hard pressed to find a way to apologize for that remark." The house shook on its old pilings as Perry stamped out. Noah glared into space. The rest of us sat there wondering whether the weekend was ruined.

"I don't think that the article is so awful," Horst said. He was Perry's lover. "She doesn't really say anything bad about anybody."

Horst was also the one in the article with AIDS. Every day at 4 A.M., he woke to blend a mixture of orange juice and AL721—a lecithin-based drug developed in Israel from egg yolks and used for AIDS treatment—because it has to be taken when there is no fat in the stomach. For a while, he would muffle the blender in a blanket but stopped, figuring that if he woke us, we would just go back to sleep. He laughed doubtfully when I told him that the blender had been invented by a man named Fred who had died recently. It was also the way he laughed when Perry phoned to say their cat had died.

Stark asked Noah, "Don't you think you were a little hard on Perry?"

Noah said, "The next thing you know, he'll be getting an agent."

I said, "We're all doing what we can, Noah. There's even a role for personalities like his."

He would look at none of us, however, so we let it go. We spoke of Noah among ourselves as not having sufficiently mourned Miguel, as if grief were a process of public concern or social responsibility, as if loss was something one just *did,* like jury duty, or going to high school. His late friend had been a leader at the beginning of the epidemic; he devised a training program for volunteers who would work with the dying; he devised systems to help others intervene for the sick in times of bureaucratic crisis. He was the first to recognize that AIDS would be a problem in prisons. A liberal priest in one of the city prisons once asked him, "Do you believe your sexuality is genetic or environmentally determined?" Miguel said, "I think of it as a calling, Father." Dead, however, Miguel could not lead; dead men don't leave footsteps in which to follow. Noah floundered.

And we all made excuses for Noah's sarcasm and inappropriate humor. He once said to someone who had put on forty pounds after starting AZT, "If you get any heavier, I won't be your pallbearer." He had known scores of others who had died before and after Miguel, helped arrange their funerals and wakes. But each death was beginning to brick him into a silo of grief, like the stones in the walls of old churches that mark the dead within.

"Let's go for a walk," his lover, Joe, said.

Noah didn't budge but their dog, Jules, came out from under a couch, a little black scottie that they had had for seventeen years. Jules began to cough, as if choking on the splintered bones of chicken carcass.

"Go for it, Bijou," Noah said. (Even the dog in our house had a drag name.) One of his bronchial tubes was collapsed, and several times a day he gagged on his own breath. He looked up at us through button eyes grown so rheumy with cataracts that he bumped into things and fell off the deck, which was actually kind of cute. Taking one of the condoms that were tossed into the shopping bag like S & H green stamps at the island grocery store, Joe rolled it down the length of Jules's tail.

"Have you ever thought of having Jules put to sleep?" Stark asked.

"Yes, but Joe won't let me," Noah said. But we knew it was Noah keeping Jules alive, or half-alive, stalling one more death.

Stark said, "I noticed that his back is sagging so much that his stomach and cock drag along the boardwalk."

"Yeah," Joe said, "but so do Noah's."

I took The Living Section containing the offending article and threw it on the stack of papers I had been accumulating all summer. My role as a volunteer was speaking to community groups about AIDS and I collected articles to keep up with all facets of the epidemic. But I had actually been saving them since they first appeared in the *Times* on a Saturday morning in July several years ago. RARE CANCER SEEN IN 41 HOMO-SEXUALS the headline of the single-column piece announced, way in the back of the paper. I read it and lowered the paper to my lap. "Uh, oh," I said.

I remember how my lover, Samuel, had asked from our bedroom, "What is it?" He was wearing a peach-colored towel around his waist, from which he would change into a raspberry-colored polo shirt and jeans. There was a swollen bruise in the crook of his arm, where he had donated plasma the day before for research on the hepatitis vaccine. As he read the article, I put the lid on the ginger jar, straightened the cushions of the sofa we had bought together, and scraped some dried substance from its plush with my thumbnail. I looked at him leaning against the door arch. He was always comfortable with his body, whether he stood or sat. Over the years, we had slipped without thinking into a monogamous relationship, and space alone competed with me for his attention. No matter where he was, space seemed to yearn for Samuel, as if he gave it definition. He once stood me in the middle of an empty stage and told me to imagine myself being projected into the entire theater. From way in the back of the house, he said, "You have a blind spot you're not filling above your right shoulder." I concentrated on that space, and he shouted, "Yes,

yes, do you feel it? That's stage presence." But I could not
sustain it the way he did.

Samuel looked up from the article. "It says here that there
is evidence to point away from contagion. None of these men
knew one another."

"But they all had other infections," I said. Hepatitis,
herpes, amebiasis—all of which I had had. Samuel used to
compare me to the Messenger in Greek tragedies, bearing news
of some plague before it hit the rest of the populace.

"It also says cytomegalovirus," he said. "What's that?"

"*Cyto* means cell; *megalo* is large," I said. "That doesn't
tell you much."

"Well, if you haven't had it," he said, "there's probably
nothing to worry about."

Perry's guest for the week came in with the day's paper, a
generous gesture, I thought, since our house's argument had
embarrassed him into leaving through the back door. His name
was Nils but we called him Mr. Norway, for that was where
he was from, and where he was a crowned and titled body-
builder. By profession, he was an anthropologist, but he pre-
ferred being observed over observing, even if the mirror was
his only audience. I didn't like him much. When he sat down
and began to read the paper I assumed he had bought for us,
I tried to admire him, since it was unlikely that I would read
the Oslo *Herald* were I in Norway. I couldn't help thinking,
however, that the steroids Nils took to achieve his award-
winning mass had made him look like a Neanderthal man. On
the other hand, I thought, perhaps that was appropriate for
an anthropologist.

I picked up the last section of the paper and turned to the
obituaries. "Gosh, there are a lot of dead people today," I said.

"You are reading the death notices every day," Nils said.
"I thought so."

"We all do," said Stark, "then we do the crossword
puzzle."

We deduced the AIDS casualties by finding the death notices of men, their age and marital status, and then their occupation. Fortunately, this information usually began the notice, or we would have been at it for hours. If the deceased was female, old, married, or worked where no one we knew would, we skipped to the next departed. A "beloved son" gave us pause, for we were all that; a funeral home was a clue, because at the time, few of them would take an AIDS casualty—those that did usually resembled our parents' refinished basements.

Stark looked over my shoulder and began at the end of the columns. "Here's a birthday message in the In Memoriams for someone who died thirty-six years ago. 'Till memory fades and life departs, you live forever in my heart.' "

"Who do people think read these things?" Enzo asked.

"I sometimes wonder if the dead have the *Times* delivered," I said.

We also looked for the neighborhood of the church where a service would be held, for we knew the gay clergy. We looked at who had bought the notice, and what was said in it. When an AIDS-related condition was not given as the cause of death, we looked for coded half-truths: cancer, pneumonia, meningitis, after a long struggle, after a short illness. The dead giveaway, so to speak, was to whom contributions could be made in lieu of flowers. Or the lyrics of Stephen Sondheim.

It was good we had this system for finding the AIDS deaths, otherwise we might have had to deal with the fact that other people were dying, too, and tragically, and young, and leaving people behind wondering what it was all about. Of course, the difference here was that AIDS was an infectious disease and many of the dead were people with whom we had had sex. We also read the death notices for anything that might connect us to someone from the past.

"Listen to this." I read, " 'Reyes, Peter. Artist and invaluable friend. Left our sides after a courageous battle. His triumphs on the stage are only footnotes to the starring role he played in our hearts. We will deeply miss you, darling, but will carry the extra richness you gave us until we build that wall again together. Contributions in his name can be made to The Three Dollar Bill Theater. Signed, The people who loved you.' "

Stark said, "You learn who your friends are, don't you?"

Horst looked thoughtfully into the near distance; his eyes watered. He said, "That is touching."

"You know what I want my death notice to read?" Enzo asked. " 'Dead GWM, loved 1950s rock and roll, Arts & Crafts ceramics, back issues of *Gourmet* magazine. Seeking similar who lived in past for quiet nights leading to long-term relationship.' "

"There's another one," Stark said, his head resting on my shoulder, his face next to mine. "Mazzochi, Robert."

"Oh, God," I said into the open wings of the newspaper.

The newsprint began to spread in runnels of ink. I handed the paper over to Stark, who read out loud, " 'Mazzochi, Robert, forty-four on July —, 1987. Son of Victor and Natalia Mazzochi of Stonington, Connecticut. Brother of Linda Mazzochi of Washington, D.C. Served as lieutenant in the United States Army. Came back from two terms of duty in Vietnam, unscarred and unblaming. With the Department of Health and Human Services NYC since 1977. A warm, radiant, much-loved man.' "

"What a nice thing to say," Horst said. "Did you know him well?"

"He was that exactly," I said.

There was another one for him, which Stark read. " 'Robert, you etched an indelible impression and left. Yes, your spirit will continue to enrich us forever, but your flesh was very particular flesh. Not a day will go by, Milton.' "

The others sat looking at me as I stood there and wept. There was Stark, an investment banker from Scotland; Horst, a mountain peasant from a farm village in Switzerland; and Enzo, who grew up in Little Italy and studied cooking in Bologna (he dressed like a street punk and spoke like a Borghese); and there was Mr. Norway on his biennial tour of gay America. They were waiting for a cue from me, some hint as to what I needed from them. I felt as if I had been spun out of time, like a kite that remains aloft over the ocean even after its string breaks. I felt awkward, out of time and out of place, like not being able to find the beat to music, which Samuel used to say that even the deaf could feel surging through the dance floor. Robert's funeral service was being held at that very moment.

The last time I had seen him was a Thursday afternoon in early October, a day of two funerals. Two friends had died within hours of one another that week. I went to the funeral of the one who had been an only child, and whose father had died before him. I went, I guess, for his mother's sake. Watching her weep was the saddest thing I had ever seen.

Afterward, I made a bargain with myself. If Robert Mazzochi was still alive, I would go to work. If he was dead, I would take the day off. When he did not answer his home phone, I called the hospital with which his doctor was associated, and the switchboard gave me his room number. I visited him on my way to work, a compromise of sorts.

"How did you know I was here?" he asked.

"Deduction."

Eggplant-colored lesions plastered his legs. Intravenous tubes left in too long had bloated his arms. Only strands were left to his mane of salt and pepper hair. He was in the hospital because thrush had coated his esophagus. The thrush irritated his diaphragm and made him hiccough so violently he could not catch his breath. Robert believed that he would have suffocated had his lover Milton not been there to perform the Heimlich maneuver. He was waiting for the nurse to bring him Demerol, which relaxed him and made it easier to breathe.

I finally said, "I can't watch you go through this."

He looked at me for a long moment. "If I've learned anything through all this, it's about hope," he said. "Hope needs firmer ground to stand on than I've got. I'm just dangling here."

" 'Nothing is hopeless. We must hope for everything,' "

I said. "That's Euripides. It's a commandment to hope. It would be a sin not to."

"Then why are you leaving me?" he asked, and I couldn't answer him. He said, "Don't worry. I am surrounded by hopeful people. Milton's hope is the most painful. But I could be honest with you."

"The truth hurts, too," I said.

"Yes, but you could take it."

"For a while."

We used to meet after work for an early supper before he went to his KS support group. One night he said to me, "I never knew that I was handsome until I lost my looks." He was still handsome as far as I was concerned, but when he pulled his wallet out to pay the check, his driver's license fell to the table. He snatched it back again, but I had seen the old picture on it, seen what must have told him that he had been a beautiful man.

The nurse came in and attached a bag of Demerol to the intravenous line feeding his arm. "We might have been lovers," Robert said to me, "if it hadn't been for Milton."

"And Samuel," I said.

The Demerol went right to his head. He closed his eyes and splayed his fingers and smiled. "My feet may never touch ground again," he said, and floated there briefly. "This is as good as it will ever get."

The rest of the day passed slowly, like a book that doesn't give one much reason to turn the page, leaving the effort all in your hands. Perry was sulking somewhere. Stark and Nils had gone to Cherry Grove. A book of Rilke's poetry, which he was not reading, lay opened on Horst's lap.

"Genius without instinct," he said during the second movement of Mozart's *Jeunehomme* piano concerto. "He knew exactly what he was doing."

"Are you all right?" I asked Enzo, who was lying in the sun, in and out of a doze.

"It's just a cold," he said. "Maybe I'll lie down for a while."

"You didn't eat breakfast today. I was watching you," I said.

"I couldn't."

"You should have something. Would you like some pasta al'burro?"

Enzo smiled. "My mother used to make that for me when I was sick."

"I could mix it with Horst's AL721. It might taste like spaghetti alla carbonara."

Horst said, "You should have some of that elixir my brother sent me from Austria. It has lots of minerals and vitamins."

"Elixir?" Enzo asked.

"That potion that's in the refrigerator."

Enzo and I worried what Horst meant by potion, for Horst went to faith healers, he had friends who were witches, he ate Chinese herbs by the fistful, and kept crystals on his bedside. These he washed in the ocean and soaked in the sun to reinvigorate them when he figured they'd been overworked. He said things like "Oh, I am glad you wore yellow today. Yellow is a healing color." Around his neck, he wore an amulet allegedly transformed from a wax-paper yogurt lid into metal by a hermit who lived in Peru, and which had been acquired by a woman who had sought him out to discuss Horst's illness. "You don't have to say anything," the hermit told her at the mouth of his cave, "I know why you're here." Fabulous line, I said to myself, that should come in handy.

Enzo and I found a silver-colored canister in the refrigerator. Its instructions were written in German, which neither of us could read. I wet a finger and stuck it in the powder. "It tastes safe," I said.

"Athletes drink it after a workout," Horst said.

"I'll have some after my nap," Enzo said.

"If you have a fever, you sweat out a lot of minerals."

"I'll mix it with cranberry juice," Enzo assured him.

"You lose a lot of minerals when you sweat," Horst said. He had been repeating himself a lot lately, as if by changing the order of the words in a sentence, he could make himself better understood.

"If you want me to cook tonight, I will," I said.

Enzo said, "The shopping's done already," and handed me a large manila envelope from the city's health department in which he kept his recipes. They were all cut from the *Times*, including the evening's menu: tuna steaks marinated in oil and herbs (herbs that Horst had growing in pots on the deck) and opma.

"What is opma?"

"It's an Indian breakfast dish made with Cream of Wheat."

"We're having a breakfast dish for dinner?" I asked.

"If this gets out, we'll be ruined socially," he said, and went to bed, leaving Horst and me alone.

Horst and I had been alone together most of the summer, except for a visit by his sister and brother, both of whom were too shy to speak whatever English they knew. Gunther cooked Horst's favorite meals. Katja dragged our mattresses, pillows, and blankets out on the deck to air. When she turned to me and said in perfect, unaccented English, "I have my doubts about Horst," I wondered how long it had taken her to put that sentence together. Gunther and I walked the beach early in the morning before Horst was up. He wanted to know all he could about Horst's prognosis, but I was afraid to tell him what I knew because I did not know what Horst wanted him to think. But fear translates, and hesitant truth translates instantly. I did not enjoy seeing them return to Switzerland, for when they thanked me for looking after their brother, I knew I had done nothing to give them hope.

"Remember my friend you met in co-op care?" I asked Horst. "He has lymphoma. The fast-growing kind."

"He should see my healer. Lymphoma is her specialty," he said. "Oh, I just remembered. Your office called yesterday. They said it was very important. Something about not getting rights for photographs. They need to put something else in your movie."

"What time did they call?"

"In the morning."

"Did you write it down?"

"No, but I remember the message. I'm sorry I forgot to tell you. I figured if it was important that they would have called back."

"They are respecting my belated mourning period," I said.

"What does this mean?"

"I'll have to go into town on Monday."

"That's too bad. How long will you stay?"

"Three or four days."

I began to look over the recipes that Enzo had handed me, angry at Horst for not telling me sooner but far more angry that I would have to leave the Island and go back to editing films I had thought were finished. Samuel had died when we were behind schedule and several hundred thousand dollars over budget on a documentary series titled *Auden in America*. Working seven-day weeks and twelve-hour days, it took a case of shingles to remind me of how much I was suffering the loss of what he had most fulfilled in me.

Perry came in while I was banging drawers and pans about the kitchen. "What's with her?" he asked Horst.

"Oh, she's got a craw up her ass," Horst said.

"I beg your pardon," I said.

"He is mad at me for not taking a message, but I say to hell with him." He raised a long, thin arm, flicked his wrist, and said, "Hoopla."

"I am not mad at you," I said, although I was. I believed that he had been using his illness to establish a system of priorities that were his alone. No one else's terrors or phone messages carried weight in his scheme of things. If he said something wasn't important, like the way he woke us up with the blender, knowing we would eventually go back to sleep, we had to take his word for it because he was dying.

And that was something we could not deny; the skeleton was rising in his face. Every two steps Death danced him backward, Horst took one forward. Death was the better dancer, and who could tell when our once-around-the-floor was next, when the terrible angel might extend a raven wing and say, "Shall we?"

And then I was angry at myself for thinking that, for elevating this thing with a metaphor. What was I doing personifying Death as a man with a nice face, a way with the girls? This wasn't a sock hop, I thought, but a Depression-era marathon with a man in a black suit who probably resembled Perry calling, "Yowsa, yowsa, yowsa, your lover's dead, your friends are dying."

As I cleared aside the kitchen counter, I came across another note in Horst's spindly handwriting. I read it out loud, " 'Sugar, your mother called. We had a nice chat. Love, Heidi.' "

"Oh, I forgot again," Horst said.

"It's all right," I said, and paused. "I'm more concerned with what you talked about."

"We talked female talk for ten minutes."

"Does that mean you talked about condoms or bathroom tiles?"

"We talked about you, too."

"What did you say?" I asked.

"I said that you were fabulous."

"Oh, good. Did you talk about . . . yourself?"

"Yes, I told her about the herb garden," he said. "I'm going to bed now for a little nap. I want to preserve my energy for tonight's supper that you are cooking." Then he went into his room and closed the door.

I looked at Perry, who registered nothing—neither about the exchange nor about the fact that his lover, who had been a bundle of energy for three days, was taking a nap.

"Aren't you out to your mother?" he asked.

"She probably knows. We just never talk about it."

"I'm surprised you don't share this part of your life with her."

"What part?" I asked.

"You shouldn't close yourself off to her, especially now."

"It wouldn't be any different if AIDS hadn't happened," I said.

"You'd have less to talk about."

"I almost called her when Samuel died."

Perry said, "I think we should get stoned and drunk together."

Horst came back out of his room. "I forgot to show you these pictures of us my sister took when I was home for harvest last time."

He showed me pictures of him and Perry carrying baskets and sitting on a tractor together. In my favorite, they were both wearing overalls, holding pitchforks, and smoking cigars.

"You two were never more handsome," I said. I looked at Perry, who pulled the joint out of his pocket. He had recently taken up smoking marijuana again after three years of health-conscious abstinence.

"Look how big my arms were then," Horst said. Then suddenly, he pounded the counter with both his fists. Everything rattled. "I hate this thing!" he said. And then he laughed at his own understatement.

"What time is dinner?" he asked.

"At nine, *liebchen*."

Horst nodded and went to bed, closing the door behind him.

Perry looked at me. I poured the vodka that was kept in the freezer while he lit the joint. I knew what was coming. It was the first time we had been alone together since Sam's death. Perry had known Sam from their days together working with a theater company for the deaf. Samuel loved sign language, which he attempted to teach me but which I would not learn, for it seemed a part of his life before we met, and I was jealous of the years I did not know him, jealous of the people as well, even the actors in their deafness, rumored to be sensuous lov-

ers. When Samuel danced, he translated the lyrics of songs
with his arms and fingers, the movement coming from his
strong, masculine back and shoulders the way a tenor sings
from his diaphragm. Sometimes I would leave the dance floor
just to watch him.

"It was easier for you," Perry said, referring to Sam's
sudden death. "It was all over for you fast."

"You make it sound as if I went to Canada to avoid the
draft."

"You didn't have to force yourself to live in hope. It's
hard to sustain all this denial."

"Maybe you shouldn't make such an effort," I said.

He looked at me. "Do you want to hear some bad news?"
Perry asked, knowing what the effect would be but unable to
resist it. The Messenger in Greek tragedies, after all, gets the
best speeches. "Bruce was diagnosed this week. PCP."

I heard a bullet intended for me pass through a younger
man's lungs. I backed away from the kitchen counter for a few
minutes, wiping my hands on a dish towel in a gesture that
reminded me of my mother.

"Are you all right?" Perry asked.

"Actually, I'm not sure how much longer I can take this."

"You're just a volunteer," he said. "I work with this on a
daily basis."

"I see," I said. "How does that make you feel when you
pay your rent?"

There are people who are good at denying their feelings;
there are those who are good at denying the feelings of others.
Perry was good at both. "Touché," he said.

"Have you ever thought about leaving the AIDS industry
for a while?" I asked him.

"I couldn't," Perry said, as if asked to perform a sexual
act he had never even imagined. "AIDS is my mission."

I finished my drink and poured myself another. "Someone
quoted Dylan Thomas in the paper the other day: 'After the
first death there is no other.' "

"What does it mean?"

"I don't know, except that I believed it once."

"We need more occasions to mourn our losses," he said.

"What do you want, Grieve-a-Thons?"

The *Times* had already done the article: "New Rituals Ease Grief as AIDS Toll Increases"; white balloons set off from courtyards; midnight cruises around Manhattan; catered affairs and delivered pizzas. It was the "bereavement group" marching down Fifth Avenue on Gay Pride Day bearing placards with the names of the dead that made me say, No, no, this has gone too far.

"I'm very distrustful of this sentimentality, this tendency toward willful pathos," I said. "A kid I met on the train was going to a bereavement counselor."

"You've become a cynic since this all began."

"That's not cynicism, that's despair."

"I haven't been of much help to you," Perry said. "I never even called to see how you were doing when you had shingles."

"I didn't need help," I said, although I had mentioned this very fact in my journal: "March 30. I am blistered from navel to spine. My guts rise and fall in waves. Noah paused a long time when I told him what I had and then asked about my health in general. Dr. Dubreuil said that shingles are not predictive of AIDS, but I know that the herpes zoster virus can activate HIV in vitro. So should that frighten me? We pin our hopes on antivirals that work in vitro. What should we fear? What should we draw hope from? What is reasonable? I worry: How much fear is choice of fear in my case? Horst has them now, as well. When I called Perry to ask him what shingles looked like, he said, 'Don't worry, if you had them, you would know it.' He hasn't called back, though the word is out."

"I have a confession to make," Perry said. "I read your journal, I mean, the Reluctant Journal."

That is what I called my diary about daily life during the epidemic: who had been diagnosed, their progress, sometimes their death. I wrote what I knew about someone who had died: what he liked in bed, his smile, his skin, the slope of his spine.

I asked Perry: "Did you read the whole thing or just the parts where your name was mentioned?"

"I read the whole thing. Out loud. To the rest of the house when you weren't here," he said. "You just went white under your tan, Blanche."

I laid the Saran Wrap over the tuna steaks that I had been preparing. The oil made the cellophane adhere to the fish in the shape of continents; the herbs were like mountain ridges on a map.

"I was just joking," Perry said.

"Right."

"You had that coming to you."

"I suppose I did."

"I don't know what to say to you about Samuel that you haven't already said to yourself," he said. "I think of him every time you enter the room. I don't know how that makes me feel about you."

"Sometimes I miss him so much I think that I am him."

I took things to the sink in order to turn my back on Perry for a moment, squaring my shoulders as I washed the double blade of the food processor's knife. What connected the two of us, I asked myself, but Samuel, who was dead? What did we have in common but illness, sexuality, death? Perry had told himself that asking me to share the house this summer was a way of getting back in touch with me after Samuel died. The truth was that he could no longer bear the sole burden of taking care of Horst. He wanted Horst to stay on the Island all summer and me to stay with him. "It would be good for you to take some time off between films, and Horst loves you," he had said, knowing all along that I knew what he was asking me to do.

Perry was silent while I washed dishes. Finally, he said, "I saw Raymond Dubreuil in co-op care last Friday night. He was still doing his rounds at midnight."

"There aren't enough doctors like him," I said, still unable to turn around.

"He works eighteen-hour days sometimes. What would happen to us if something should happen to him?"

"I asked him what he thought about that *Times* article that said an infected person had a greater chance of developing AIDS the longer they were infected. Ray said the reporter made years of perfect health sound worse than dying within eighteen months of infection."

Perry had brought up a larger issue and placed it between us like a branch of laurel. I turned around. His hand was on the counter, middle two fingers folded under and tucked to the palm, his thumb, index, and little finger extended in the deaf's sign for "I love you." But he did not raise his hand. I thought of Auden's lines from *The Rake's Progress,* "How strange! Although the heart dare everything/ The hand draws back and finds no spring of courage." For a passing moment, I loathed Perry, and I think the feeling was probably mutual. He had what I was certain was a damaged capacity to love.

Joe came in followed by Stark and Nils. Joe kissed me and put his arm around my shoulder. "Nils told me a friend of yours died. I'm sorry. Are you okay?"

Perry slapped the counter.

"Don't get me started," I said. "Where's Noah?"

"We've been visiting a friend with a pool," Joe said. "Here's something for your diary. This guy just flew all the way to California and back to find a psychic who would assure him that he won't die of AIDS."

"Why didn't he just get the antibody test?" I asked.

"Because if it came out positive, he'd commit suicide. Anyway, Noah's coming to take you to tea. Where's Enzo?"

Stark came out of the room he shared with Enzo. "His body's there, but I can't attest to anything else. Does this mean you're cooking dinner?"

Nils came out of my room, which had the guest bed in it. He had changed into a pastel-colored muscle shirt bought in the Grove. I stiffened as he put an arm around me. "Come to tea and I will buy you a drink," Nils said.

"We'll be there soon," Perry said in a tone that implied wounds from the morning were being healed. Nils left to save us a place before the crowd got there. While the others were getting ready, Perry began to scour the kitchen counter. Someone was always cleaning the sink or dish rack for fear of bacteria or salmonella, mainly because of Horst, but you never know. Perry asked, "You don't like Nils, do you?"

"No. He has ingrown virginity."

"Meaning he wouldn't put out for you?"

"And another thing . . . all I've heard this week is that the Pines is going to tea later, that we're eating earlier, that there's more drag, fewer drugs, more lesbians, and less sexual tension. For an anthropologist, he sounds like *The New York Times*."

Noah's long, slow steps could be heard coming around the house. When he saw Perry in the kitchen, he stopped in the center of the deck. Noah looked at Perry, raised his eyebrows, then turned and entered the house through the sliding door of his and Joe's room. Perry turned to the mirror and ran a comb through his mustache. From a tall vase filled with strings of pearls bought on Forty-second Street for a dollar, he selected one to wrap around his wrist. The pearls were left over from the previous summer, when the statistics predicting the toll on our lives were just beginning to come true; there were dozens of strands, in white, off-white, the colors of after-dinner mints. This will be over soon, my friend Anna says, they will find a cure, they have to. I know what she is saying. When it began, we all thought it would be over in a couple of years; perhaps the *Times* did as well, and did not report on it much, as if the new disease would blow over like a politician's sex scandal. AIDS to them was what hunger is to the fed, something we think we can imagine because we've been on a diet.

From behind the closed door of their bedroom, I heard Joe whisper loudly to Noah, "You're not going to change anything by being angry at him." Perry stared at the door for a moment as if he should prepare to bolt. Instead, he asked, "Are you still mad at me about the article?"

"I never was."

"But you were angry."

I looked over at the stack of papers accumulating near the couch, only then beginning to wonder what I achieved by saving them, what comfort was to be gained. "I always expect insight and consequence from their articles, and I'm disappointed when they write on our issues and don't report more than what we already know," I said. "And sometimes I assume that there is a language to describe what we're going through, and that they would use it if there was."

"You should have told me about your friend," Perry said.

"This is one I can't talk about," I said. "As for your suggestion . . . I don't know how I would begin to tell my mother about my life as I know it now."

"You could say, 'I've got some good news and some bad news.'"

"What's the good news?"

"You don't have AIDS."

Noah was still taking a shower when the others left for tea. He came out of the bathroom with an oversized towel wrapped around his waist and lotion rubbed into his face and hands. I could see the tiny scar on his back where the liposuction surgery had vacuumed a few pounds of fat. Tall and mostly bald, older than he would confess to, he was certainly as old as he looked. For a moment, he regarded me as if I were a dusty sock found under the bed. Then his face ripened.

"Dish alert," he said. "Guess who's having an affair with a twenty-two year-old and I'm not supposed to tell anyone?"

"Perry," I said almost instantly. "The bastard."

"They were together in Washington for the international AIDS conference, supposedly in secret, but word has gotten back that they were making out in public like a couple of Puerto Rican teenagers on the subway."

"Does Horst know?"

"Of course. Perry thinks that talking about dishonest behavior makes it honest. As far as I'm concerned, it's another distraction from Horst's illness. Perry distanced himself from everyone when it became obvious that they were dying. Last year it was Miguel, this year it's Horst. When I confronted him, he said, 'Don't deny me my denial.' "

"Oh, that's brilliant. As long as he claims to be in denial, he doesn't even have to appear to suffer," I said. "One of these days, all this grief he's avoiding is going to knock him on his ass."

"But then he'll wear it around town like an old cloth coat so that everyone will feel sorry for him. He won't be happy until people in restaurants whisper 'Brava' as he squeezes past them to his table."

"What's the boyfriend like?"

"What kind of person has an affair with a man whose lover is dying of AIDS?" Noah asked.

I said, "The kind that probably splits after the funeral."

"He's what my Aunt Gloria would call a mayonnaise Jew, someone trying to pass for a WASP."

"I don't know if I should be offended by that or not," I said.

"But get this: He's had three lovers since he graduated from Harvard. The first one's lover died of AIDS. The second one had AIDS. Now there's Perry. So this kid gets the antibody test. It came back negative, and now he's got survivor's guilt." Noah gave me one of his bland, expressionless looks. "Perry acts as if this were the most misunderstood love affair since Abélard and Héloïse. He told me it was one of those things in life you just have no control over."

"For someone so emotionally adolescent, he's gotten a lot of mileage out of this epidemic," I said.

"Where else would he be center stage with a degree in drama therapy?" Noah asked. "He even quoted your journal at the last AIDS conference."

"What?"

"In Washington. He quoted you in a paper he presented. I knew he hadn't told you yet," Noah said. "He was certain you'd be honored. He would have been."

"Do you know what he used?"

"Something about an air of pain, the cindered chill of loss. It was very moving. You wondered if there wasn't a hidden cost to constant bereavement. You know Perry, he probably presented your diary as the work of a recent widower whose confidentiality had to be protected. That way he didn't have to give you credit."

I once went to an AIDS conference. Perry treated them like summer camp—Oh, Mary, love your hat, let's have lunch. I had seen him deliver papers that were barely literate and unprepared, and what was prepared was plagiarized. Claiming he was overwhelmed with work, he feigned modesty and said he could only speak from his heart. When social scientists provided remote statistics on our lives, Perry emoted and confessed. "My personal experience is all I can offer as the essence of this presentation." And it worked. It gave everyone the opportunity to cry and feel historic.

Noah asked, "Are you coming to tea? There's someone I want you to meet."

"Another widower?" I asked. "More damaged goods?"

"I'll put it to you this way," Noah said, "you have a lot in common."

With regard to human affairs, Noah was efficient. "Let me count the ways," I said, "a recent death, the ache of memory, reduced T-cell functions, positive sero status . . ."

"Yes, well, there's that."

"And maybe foreshortened futures, both of us wary of commitment should one or the other get sick, the dread of taking care of someone else weighed against the fear of being sick and alone."

"I doubt that Samuel would like your attitude."

"Samuel will get over it," I said. "And I'm not interested in a relationship right now. I'm only interested in sex."

"Safer sex, of course."

"I want to wake up alone, if that's what you mean."

Noah raised his eyebrows and lowered them again, as if to say that he would never understand me. I said, "Let me tell you a story. I hired a Swedish masseur recently because I wanted to be touched by someone, and no one in particular, if you get my innuendo. At one point, he worked a cramped muscle so hard that I cried out. And he said, 'That's it, go ahead, let it out'—as if I was holding something back, you know, intellectualizing a massage. I asked him if he felt anything, and he said, 'I feel'—long pause—'sorrow.' I told him that I had been a little blue lately but it wasn't as bad as all that."

Noah nodded. He said, "The real reason I didn't want to be interviewed for the piece in the *Times* was because Perry invited the reporter for dinner and told her we'd all get into drag if she brought a photographer."

Before I went down to the beach, I looked in on Enzo. Stark was right. The only time I'd ever seen anyone like this before was when Horst was first diagnosed. Perry had scheduled people just to sit with him, when none of us thought he would even survive. Enzo's skin was moist, his lips dry, his breath light. He was warm, but not enough for alarm.

These summer evenings I sat on the beach in a sling-back chair, listening to my cassette player and writing things about Samuel. I recalled our life together backward. The day he went into the hospital, he had cooked himself something to eat and left the dishes in the sink. Then he was dead, and washing his dishes was my last link to him as a living being. This evening, the pages of my journal felt like the rooms of my apartment when I came home and found it burglarized. Like my apartment, I knew I had to either forsake it or reclaim it as my own. Though in this case something had been taken, nothing was missing. I was angry with Perry, but it was not the worst thing he could have done. The worst is not when we can say it is the worst.

I started to write about Robert. The words of his obituary, "warm, radiant, much-loved man," somewhat assuaged my remorse at having abandoned him to the attention of the more hopeful. The beach was nearly empty at this time of the day —as it was in the morning—except for those like me who were drawn by the light of the early evening, the color of the water, the sand, the houses seen without the protection of sunglasses. Others passed and I nodded from my beach chair. We smiled. Everyone agreed that the Island was friendlier this year, as if nothing were at stake when we recognized one another's existence. Verdi's Requiem was on my Walkman, a boat was halfway between the shore and the horizon. One full sail pulled the boat across the halcyon surface of the water. Near me a man stood with his feet just in the waves. He turned and held his binoculars as if he were offering me a drink. "They're strong," he said. I found the sailboat in the glasses. I found a handsome and popular Episcopal priest who I knew from experience to be a fine lover in bed. He was in collar and was praying. There was another handsome man. He was indistinct but I recognized his expression. He reached into a box and released his fist over the boat's rail. Another man and a woman repeated the gesture. *Libera me.* The surviving lover shook the entire contents of the cloth-wrapped box overboard. The winds that spin the earth took the ashes and grains of bones and spilled them on the loden-green sea. He was entirely gone now but for the flecks that stuck to their clothes and under their nails, but for the memory of him, and for the pleasure of having known him. The boaters embraced with that pleasure so intense they wept at it. *Dies magna et amara valde.* I returned the binoculars to the man. It was a beautiful day and it was wonderful to be alive.

PART II

Two old couches, one ersatz wicker, the other what my mother used to call colonial, sat at a right angle to one another in the middle of our living room. Enzo and Horst were lying on them with their heads close together, like conspiring convalescents. Horst's cheeks were scarlet.

"You aren't feeling well, are you?" I asked.

Horst said, "No, but I didn't want to tell Perry and spoil his weekend."

"How is Enzo doing?"

"He thinks he has a cold, but I don't think so."

From where I stood, I could lay my hand on both their foreheads. I felt like a television evangelist. Enzo's forehead was the warmer of the two.

"I hear there's a flu going around," Horst said.

"Where did you hear that? You haven't been in town in a week."

"I had a flu shot," he said. "I think I'm not worried."

Without opening his eyes, Enzo said, "You had better get started if you are going to cook supper before everyone gets back. I put all the ingredients out for you."

I heated oil as the recipe instructed. "When the oil is very hot add mustard seeds," it read. "Keep the lid of the pan handy should the seeds sputter and fly all over." In the first grade, I recalled giving a girl named Karen Tsakos a mustard-seed bracelet in a Christmas exchange, selecting it myself from the dollar rack at a store called Gaylord's. "Aren't mustard seeds supposed to be a symbol of something?" I asked as they began to explode between me and the cabinet where the lids were kept.

"Hope, I think," Enzo said.

"Perhaps I should put more in."

"No, faith," Horst said, lying down in his bedroom.

"Faith is a fine invention, as far as I can see, but microscopes are prudent, in case of emergency," I said, approximating a poem by Emily Dickinson. Horst laughed, but Enzo showed no sign whatsoever that he knew what I was talking about. I wasn't so sure myself what Dickinson meant by an emergency: Could a microscope confirm one's belief in a crisis of faith, or, in a crisis of nature, such as an epidemic illness, was man best left to his own devices?

"How's dinner coming?" Stark asked, returning five minutes before it was to have been on the table.

"It's not ready," I said.

"Why not?"

"I didn't start it in time," I said.

"Why not?"

"Because I was at a funeral."

He picked up one of Miguel's old porno magazines and disappeared into the bathroom with it. He emerged ten minutes later and asked, "Is there anything I could be doing?"

"You can light the coals, and grill the tuna steaks. I've got to watch the opma," I said. "Enzo, what are gram beans?"

"The little ones."

Perry returned next and kissed me. "I forgot to tell you that Luis is in the hospital again," he said loudly. "His pancreas collapsed but he seems to be getting better."

"Enzo, I think I burned the gram beans."

"Luis's lover, Dennis, just took the antibody test," Perry said. "He was sero-negative."

"Oh, that's good."

"Yeah. Luis said, 'Thank God for hemorrhoids.' "

"Enzo, which of these is the cumin?"

"Don't cumin my mouth," Perry said, going into his room to check on Horst. I watched him brush the hair off Horst's forehead and take the thermometer out of Horst's mouth to kiss him. Perry's face darkened when he read the thermometer, as if he didn't know what to think. I added the Cream of Wheat to the gram beans.

Nils came up to me and wrapped a huge arm around my shoulder. "They told me down at tea that if dinner was scheduled for nine, that meant ten in Fire Island time."

"Dinner would have been ready at nine o'clock if I hadn't been given this god-awful recipe to make," I said, sounding more angry than I intended, and Nils hastened away. Noah came to the stove. "You are bitter, aren't you?"

"He's like Margaret Mead on steroids," I said.

"He's writing a book," Noah said.

"Yeah, sure, *Coming of Age in Cherry Grove*."

"What's this here?" Noah asked.

"Opma."

"Where did you get the recipe?"

"From *The New York Times*."

"I hate that paper."

Stark came running into the kitchen with the tuna steaks and put them in the electric broiler. The recipe said to grill them four minutes on each side.

"The grill will never get hot enough," he said. "Is that opma?"

"In the flesh."

"It looks like Cream of Wheat with peas in it."

Noah found the radio station we always listened to during dinner on Saturday nights. "Clark, what's the name of this song?" he asked, a game we played as part of the ritual. Enzo usually played along as he did the cooking.

" 'The Nearness of You,' " I answered.

"Who's singing?"

"Julie London."

"Who wrote it?"

"Johnny Mercer." Enzo didn't say anything, though the correct answer was Hoagy Carmichael. Perry sang as he helped Joe set the table, making up his own lyrics as he went along, the way a child does, with more rhyme than reason. We were all aware that he and Noah were behaving as if the other were not in the room, but their orbits were getting closer. As the song closed, Perry and I turned to one another and imitated the deep voice of the singer: "It's just the queerness of you." Then I made everyone laugh by stirring the thickening opma with both hands on the spoon. Jules, the dog, began hacking in the center of the room.

"Did you have a productive cough, dear?" Joe asked. Horst laughed from his bedroom.

"Enzo, come tell me if the opma is done," I said. He kind of floated up off the couch as if he was pleasantly drunk. I knew then that he was seriously ill. He took the wooden spoon from me and poked the opma twice. "It's done," he said.

We went to the table. I sat in the center, with Enzo on my right, Nils across from me, Joe on my left. Perry and Noah faced each other from the opposite ends, like parents. This was how we sat, each and every week. The guest was always in the same chair, whether he knew it or not. For the first several minutes of dinner, the table was a tangle of large arms passing the salad and popping open beer cans.

"Eat something, darling," I said to Enzo, who was only staring at the fish on his plate. "You haven't eaten anything all day."

Perry said, "This is the best opma I ever had."

Horst looked up as if he had something to announce, his fork poised in the air. We all turned to him. His fork fell to his plate with a clatter, and he said, "I think I have to lie down."

Perry said, "This opma will taste good reheated."

"So Fred told me this story at tea about the last of the police raids on the Meat Rack in the early seventies," Noah said.

"You're going to love this, Clark," Perry said.

"The cops came in one night with huge flashlights and handcuffs. There were helicopters and strobe lights; they had billy clubs and German shepherds. And they started dragging away dozens of men. The queens were crying and screaming and pleading with the cops because they would get their names in the paper and lose their jobs, you know, this was when it was still illegal for two men to dance with one another. The guys that got away hid under the bushes until everything was clear. Finally, after everything was perfectly quiet, some queen whispered, 'Mary, Mary!' And someone whispered back, 'Shhh, no names!' "

"Nils, would you like this?" Enzo asked. I looked up at Nils, whose forearms circled his plate. Everyone looked at me looking at him. I picked up Enzo's tuna steak with my fork and dropped it on Nils's plate. Enzo got up and stumbled to the couch.

Stark and Joe cleared the table. Perry went outside and smoked a cigar. With his back turned toward the house, he was calling attention to himself. I sat on the arm of the couch, looking down at Enzo and looking out at Perry, wondering who needed me most. But Noah was also looking at Perry. I could see him in his room, a finger on his lip, looking through the doors that opened out onto the deck. He stepped back from my sight and called, "Perry, this doesn't fit me. Would you like to try it on?"

The next thing I knew, Perry was wearing a black velvet Empress gown, like the one Madame X wears in the Sargent painting. In one hand, he held its long train, in the other, a cigar. Between the cleavage of the dress was Perry's chest hair, the deepest part of which was gray.

"Where'd you get that dress?" Stark asked.

"Noah inherited Miguel's hope chest. It was in the will."

Enzo was smiling, but I knew he was faking it. I whispered, "Do you need help to your bed?"

He clutched my hand and I helped him into his room. His forehead was scalding. "I'll be right back," I told him. I ran into the kitchen and pulled a dish towel from the refrigerator handle and soaked it under cold water. By this time, Noah was wearing the silver-lined cape that went with Perry's gown, a Frederick's of Hollywood merry widow, and silver lamé high heels. On his bald head was a tiny silver cap. I smiled as I passed through them, but they didn't see me.

Horst was sitting on Enzo's bed when I got back to him. This was the room in which Miguel had died the year before, and which Horst did not want this summer, though it was bigger and cooler than his own room and its glass doors opened onto the deck. "I could hear his breathing over all the commotion," Horst said. "Have you taken any aspirin?"

"I've been taking aspirin, Tylenol, and Advil every two hours," Enzo said, his voice strengthened by fear's adrenaline.

Horst asked, "Did you take your temperature?"

"I don't have a thermometer."

Horst got his own. "I cleaned it with peroxide," he said. "I hope that is good enough." Before I could ask him how to use it, he was on his way back to bed.

I pulled the thermometer from its case, pressed a little button, and placed it in Enzo's mouth. Black numbers pulsed against a tiny gray screen. I watched its numbers climb like a scoreboard from hell. Outside, Nils's arms were flailing because the high heels he was wearing were stuck between the boards of the deck. The thermometer beeped. Perry and Noah, in full drag, walked off with Nils between them.

"You have a temperature of a hundred and three point two," I said. This was the first time in my life I had ever been able to read a thermometer. "Do you want me to get the Island doctor?"

"Let's see if it goes down. Can you get me some cranberry juice?"

I went into the kitchen. Stark and Joe were reading. "How's he doing?" Joe asked.

"I think we should get him to a doctor."

"The number's on the ferry schedule," Joe said, and went back to his book.

A machine at the doctor's office said in the event of an emergency, to leave a number at the sound of the beep. I could not imagine the doctor picking up messages that late at night. But what I really feared was the underlying cause of Enzo's fever. I put the phone in its cradle.

"Don't we know any doctors?" I asked.

Stark and Joe shook their heads. Joe said that Noah or Perry might. I suddenly realized how isolated the Island was at night. At this point, there was no way of getting Enzo off the Island short of a police helicopter.

He was asleep when I took him his juice. He was not the handsomest of men, but at this moment he was downright homely. He cooked all our meals for us, meals to which even Horst's fickle appetite responded. He overstocked the refrigerator with more kinds of foodstuff than we could identify. We wondered why he did it, even as we stored away a few extra pounds, telling ourselves we were delaying the sudden weight loss associated with the first signs of AIDS. Perry had put on so much weight, his posture changed. He tilted forward as he walked. If he should develop the AIDS-associated wasting-away syndrome, Noah told him, months might go by before anyone would notice. I took the towel off Enzo's head and soaked it in cold water again.

"You'll be sure to clean Horst's thermometer before you give it back to him," he said, holding my hand, which held the towel to his face.

"Yes, of course."

"I mean it."

"Let me take your temperature again. This thermometer is really groovy." His temperature had risen to just shy of 104. With all I knew about AIDS, I suddenly realized I did not even know what this meant. "When was the last time you took some aspirin?"

"An hour ago. I'll give it another one."

The house shook as Perry, Noah, and Nils returned, all aglow with the success of their outing. Perspiration hung off Perry's chest hair like little Italian lights strung about the Tavern on the Green. Nils got into a clean tank top and went dancing.

Noah snapped open a Japanese fan and waved it at his face. "Dish alert," he said. He could be charming. For a moment, I forgot Enzo, the thermometer in my hand.

Joe said, "Clark thinks Enzo needs a doctor."

Noah asked, "What's his temperature?"

I stood in the doorway. "It's one hundred and four," I said, exaggerating a little.

"That's not too bad."

"It isn't?"

"Is he delirious?" Noah asked.

"What if he's too sick to be delirious?"

Perry said, "Miguel's temperature used to get much higher than that. He'd be ranting and raving in there sometimes."

"Yes, but Miguel is dead," I said.

When we opened the house this summer, I threw away his sheets, the polyester bathrobes, the towels from Beth Israel, St. Vincent's, Sloan-Kettering, and Mt. Sinai that filled our closets and dresser drawers from all of Miguel's hospital visits. Noah had watched me, neither protesting nor liking what I was doing. But I could not conceive of any nostalgia that would want to save such souvenirs. The hospital linen was part and parcel of the plastic pearls, the battery-operated hula doll, the Frederick's of Hollywood merry widow, five years' worth of porno magazine subscriptions, the measure of the extremes they went to for a laugh last year, the last summer of Miguel's life. Why did we need them when we were still getting post-dated birthday presents from Miguel: sweaters on our birthday, Smithfield hams at Christmas, magazine subscriptions in his name care of our address—anything he could put on his Visa card once he realized that he would expire before it did.

"If Enzo's temperature gets too high, we can give him an alcohol bath, or a shower, to bring it down," Noah said.

"So can I go to bed now?" Stark asked.

"Sure," I said. "Just don't sleep too soundly."

I went into my own room, which smelled of Nils's clothes, his sweat and the long trip, of coconut suntan lotion and the salty beach. I missed Samuel at moments like this, missed his balance of feelings, of moderated emotions as if he proportioned them out, the pacifying control he had over me. I fell asleep, woke and listened for Enzo's breath, and fell asleep again. I halfway woke again and sensed my longing even before

Nils's presence woke me completely. In the next bed, a sheet pulled up to his nipples, Nils's chest filled the width of the bed.

Drunk one night on the beach, he had said to me, "Perry doesn't think there's hope for anyone who is diagnosed in the next few years."

"We've pinned our hopes on so many," I said, aware that Nils was delving for useful information, "that I don't know what role hope plays anymore. They're predicting as many deaths in 1991 alone as there were Americans killed in Vietnam. Some of those are bound to be people one knows."

"Hope is the capacity to live with the uncertain," he said.

I had read that line myself somewhere. "Bullshit," I said. Nils stepped back and looked at me as if I had desecrated the theology of some deified psychotherapist.

"You don't need hope to persevere," I said.

"What do you need, then?" Nils asked.

"Perseverance," I answered, and laughed at myself. And then I told him a story I had heard at a funeral service. It was the story of an Hassidic rabbi and a heckler. The rabbi had told his congregation that we must try to put everything into the service of God, even that which was negative and we didn't like. The heckler called out, "Rabbi, how do we put a disbelief in God into His service?" The rabbi's answer made me think that God and hope are interchangeable. He told the heckler, "If a man comes to you in a crisis, do not tell him to have faith, that God will take care of everything. Act instead as if God does not exist. Do what you can do to help the man."

Nils put his arm around me and pulled me up close to him as we walked. There was a strong wind that night, and the waves were high. The moon was low across the water and illuminated the waves as they reached for it. I felt massive muscles working in Nils's thighs and loins, a deep and deeper mechanism than I had ever felt in a human body, and which seemed to have as its source of energy that which lifted the waves and kept the moon suspended. He was that strong, and

I would feel that secure. A bulwark against the insentient night, his body: if I did not need hope to persevere, I needed that. He stopped and held me, kissed my head politely, and pushed me out at arms' length. He made me feel like the canary sent down the mine to warn him of dangerous wells of feeling, wells that he could draw upon but needn't descend himself.

When I woke again, the oily surface of his back was glowing. The sky held more prophecy than promise of light. I got up to check on Enzo. He was not in bed. Stark was sitting up waiting for him to come out of the bathroom. He patted the bed next to him. I sat down and he put his arm around me.

"Has he been sleeping?" I asked.

"Like the dead."

"Do you think we should have gotten a helicopter off the Island?"

"No, but I wish we had."

Enzo could be heard breathing through the thin door. Stark said, "It's been like that all night."

The toilet flushed, we heard Enzo moan, then the thud of his body falling against the bathroom door.

Stark carefully pushed it opened and looked in. "All hell broke loose," he said.

Enzo was lying in a puddle of excrement. In his delirium, he had forgotten to pull his pajamas down before sitting on the toilet. When he tried to step out of them, his bowels let go a spray of watery stool. His legs were covered, as were the rugs and the wall against which he fainted.

"You're burning up, darling," Stark whispered to him.

"I'm afraid he'll dehydrate," I said.

I pulled off Enzo's soiled pajamas, turned the shower on, and took off the old gym shorts I slept in. "Hand him over," I said from within the lukewarm spray.

Enzo wrapped his arms around my back and laid his hot head on my shoulder. Our visions of eternal hell must come from endless febrile nights like this, I thought. I gradually made the water cooler and sort of two-stepped with him so that it would run down his back, and sides, and front. The shower spray seemed to clothe our nakedness. If I closed my eyes, we were lovers on a train platform. We could have been almost anywhere, dancing in the sad but safe aftermath of some other tragedy, say the Kennedy assassinations, the airlift from Saigon, the bombing of a Belfast funeral. Stark used the pump bottle of soap—bought to protect Horst from whatever bacteria, fungus, or yeast might accumulate on a shared bar—to lather Enzo's legs. I slowly turned the water cooler.

"Can we get your head underwater a little bit?" I asked, though Enzo was barely conscious. "Let's see if we can get your fever down."

"I think we're raising it," Stark murmured. He was washing Enzo's buttocks and his hand would reach through Enzo's legs and wash his genitals almost religiously. He reached through Enzo's legs and lathered my genitals as well. He pulled on my testicles and loosened them in their sack. He pulled and squeezed them just to the pleasure point of pain. He winked at me but he didn't smile. I noticed there were interesting shampoos on the shelf that I had never tried.

"I can't stand much longer, you guys," Enzo whispered in my ear. "I'm sorry."

I maneuvered him around to rinse the soap off. Stark waited with huge towels. While I dried us both, Stark changed Enzo's bedclothes, tucking the fresh sheets in English style. Then he helped me carry him back to bed.

"Let's take his temperature before he falls asleep," I said. Stark stared in my face as we waited. The thermometer took so long, I was afraid it was broken. It finally went off with a tremulous beep. "Dear God," I said.

"What is it?"

Despite the shower, his fever was over 105. "Do we have any rubbing alcohol?" I asked.

Stark couldn't find any after checking both bathrooms. I said, "Get the vodka, then."

He returned with the ice-covered bottle from the freezer; the liquor within it was gelatinous. "Do you think this wise?" he asked.

"Not the imported. Get the stuff we give the guests. Wait," I said. "Leave that one here and bring me a glass."

Stark brought the domestic vodka and a sponge. "Do you know what you're doing?" he asked.

"Alcohol brings a temperature down by rapidly evaporating off the body," I said. "Vodka happens to evaporate faster than rubbing alcohol. Other than that, no, I don't have the faintest idea."

Stark watched me for a while, then took Enzo's temperature himself. It had fallen to 104.8. "I think we should get some aspirin in him," he said, which we woke Enzo to do. He drank a little juice. Fifteen minutes later, I took his temperature again. Enzo's temperature had gone down to 104.6. While waiting for this reading, Stark had fallen back to sleep. I wondered whether he didn't want me in bed with him. That would have been pleasant, temporary; he was a solid man, like a park bench.

But instead, I went out to the living room. My stack of newspapers was near the couch. I could look in on Enzo if I clipped the articles I intended to save. Just the night before, Noah had shaken his head at all the papers and said, "It looks like poor white trash lives here."

"My roots must be showing," I said.

I clipped my articles and put them in an accordion file that I kept closed with an old army-issue belt. Sometimes margin notes reminded me why I was saving something, such as the obituary of an interior designer, in which, for the first time, the lover was mentioned as a survivor. Or the piece in which being sero-positive for HIV antibodies became tantamount to HIV infection, indicating that our language for talking about AIDS was changing. "With the passage of time, scientists are beginning to believe that all those infected will develop symptoms and die," the article said. It really doesn't sit well to read about one's mortality in such general terms.

In the magazine section, a popular science writer wrote that there was no moral message in AIDS. Over the illustration, I scrawled, "When late is worse than never." Scientists had been remiss, he said, for "viewing it as a contained and peculiar affliction of homosexual men." In the margin I wrote, "How much did they pay you to say this?"

Then there were those living-out-loud columns written by a woman who had given up on actual journalism to raise her children. Some of them were actually quite perceptive, but I had never forgiven her for the one in which the writer confessed that she had been berated by a gay man in a restaurant for saying, "They were so promiscuous—no wonder they're dying."

Horst emerged from his bedroom to blend his AL721, which was kept in the freezer in ice-cube trays. He did not see me and I did not say anything for fear of frightening him because he concentrated so severely on his task. If you did not know him, you would not think he was ill, but very, very old. He had always been a vulnerable and tender man, but now he was fragile. He hoped that the elixir in his blender could keep the brush of death's wings from crushing him entirely.

When Samuel called to tell me two years ago that Horst had been diagnosed, I began to weep mean, fat tears. My assistant editor sent me out for a walk. I wandered aimlessly around SoHo for a while, once trying to get into the old St. Patrick's, its small walled-in cemetery covered with the last of autumn's spongy brown leaves. I fingered cowhide and pony pelts hanging in a window; I bought a cheap stopwatch from a street vendor, some blank tapes, and spare batteries for my tape cassette. Eventually, hunger made me find a place to rest, a diner with high ceilings and windows looking onto a busy street. After I ordered, I thought of Horst again, and something odd happened: the room—no, not the room, but my vision went, like after you've looked at the sun too long. All I could see was a glowing whiteness, like a dentist's lamp, or the inside of a Nautilus shell. For a brilliant moment, I saw nothing, and knew nothing, but this whiteness that had anesthetized and cauterized the faculties by which one savors the solid world. Like a film dissolving from one scene to another, the room came back, but the leftover whiteness limned the pattern of one man's baldness, glittered off the earring of his companion, turned the white shirt my waitress wore to porcelain, fresh and rigid, as it was from the Chinese laundry. She stood over me with a neon-bright plate in one hand and the beer's foam glowing in the other, waiting for me to lift my elbows and give her room to put down my lunch.

"Oh, shit," Horst said, knocking the orange-juice carton over and spilling some into the silverware drawer.

"I'll clean it up," I said softly.

"I knew you were there," he said. "I heard you in here. How is Enzolina?"

"His temperature was very high. We got it down a little bit."

"You must sleep, too." He leaned over me and kissed my cheek. "It's okay about Perry and his boyfriend," he said, obviously having heard Noah speaking that afternoon. "Perry is still affectionate and he takes care of me. And I don't feel so sexual anymore. But Noah shouldn't have told you, because it would only make you angry."

Whether it was the lateness of the hour or the sensitive logic of pain, I thought I heard resignation in Horst's voice, as if he were putting one foot in the grave just to test the idea of it.

"Have you met the boyfriend?"

"Oh, yes. He's very bland. I don't know what Perry sees in him," Horst said. "Perry thinks the three of us should go into therapy together, but I'm not doing it. I don't have to assuage their guilt."

"Where will Perry be when you get really sick?"

"Probably at a symposium in Central Africa." He laughed and waved his hand like an old woman at an off-color joke. Horst used to be hardy, real peasant stock. He was the kind of man who could wear a ponytail and make it look masculine.

Here was a man gang-banged for four days by a bunch of Turks on the Orient Express who lived to turn the memory into a kind of mantra. He said, "Perry needs so many buffers from reality."

"Most of us do."

"Not you."

"You're wrong," I said. Then I showed him the article on the death of an iconoclastic theater director that had started on the front page of the *Times*. "Look, there's a typo. It says he died of AIDS-related nymphoma."

He laughed and laid his head in my lap. "I am homesick for Switzerland," he said. "I'd like to go home, but I don't know if I could handle the trip. And I don't want to be a burden on my family."

"You wouldn't be."

"I've been thinking lately I don't want to be cremated. I want to be buried in the mountains. But it's so expensive."

"Horst, don't worry about expenses," I said.

"How is Samuel?" he asked.

"He's dead, honey. He died this winter."

"Oh, I'm sorry," he said, and covered his face with his hands. Memory lapses are sometimes part of the deterioration. I wondered whether Perry had noticed or ignored them. "I forget these things," he added.

"It's late, you're tired." He started up. I said, "Horst, I think you should go home if you want to. Just make sure you come back."

My fingertips were pungent with the smell of newsprint, like cilantro, or the semen smell of ailanthus seeds in July. "Did you see that piece in today's paper?" we asked one another over the phone when a point we held dear was taken up on the editorial page. "Yes, haven't they come far and in such a short time," we responded. I filed it all away, with little science and what was beginning to feel like resignation: *C* for condoms, *S* for Heterosexuals, *P* for Prevention and Safer Sex, *R* for Race and Minorities, *O* for Obits.

"I can't tell you how bored I am with this," a man said to me on the beach one evening when he learned that another friend had gone down for the count. He said, "Sometimes I wish there was something else to talk about," which is what my mother used to say as she put her makeup on for a night out with my father. "I just wish we could go out and talk about anything but you kids and the house," she'd say with the vague longing I recall with numbing resonance. "I just wish there was something else to talk about."

They would eat at a place called D'Amico's Steak House, where the menus were as large as parking spaces. She would have frogs' legs, which she told me tasted like chicken, but were still a leap toward the exotic, no matter how familiar the landing. Her desire had no specific object; she was not an educated woman; she did not even encourage fantasy in her children; but it still arouses whatever Oedipal thing there is left unresolved in me, and I often wish to be able to satisfy it—to give her nights and days of conversation so rooted in the present that no reference to when we were not happy could ever be made, and no dread of what to come could be imagined. But we both know that there's no forgetting that we were once unhappy. Our conversation is about my sisters' lives and their children. She ends our infrequent telephone conversations with "Please take care of yourself," emphasizing, without naming, her fear of losing me to an illness we haven't talked about, or to the ebbs of time and its hostilities that have carried me further and further away from perfect honesty with her.

But language also takes you far afield. Metaphors adumbrate; facts mitigate. For example, "Nothing is hopeless; we must hope for everything." I had believed this until I realized the lie of its intrinsic metaphor, that being without hope is not being, plunged into the abyss that nothingness fills. We have not come far since the world had one language and few words. Babel fell before we had a decent word for death, and then we were numb, shocked at the thought of it, and this lisping dumb word—*death, death, death*—was the best we could come up with.

And simply speak, disinterested and dryly, the words that fill your daily life: "Lewis has KS of the lungs," or "Raymond has endocarditis but the surgeons won't operate," or "Howard's podiatrist will not remove a bunion until he takes the test," or "Cytomegalovirus has inflamed his stomach and we can't get him to eat," or "The DHPG might restore the sight in his eye," or "The clinical trial for ampligen has filled up," or "They've added dementia to the list of AIDS-related illnesses," or "The AZT was making him anemic," or "His psoriasis flaked so badly, the maid wouldn't clean his room," or "They found tuberculosis in his glands," or "It's a form of meningitis carried in pigeon shit; his mother told him he should never have gone to Venice," or "The drug's available on a compassionate basis," or "The drug killed him," or "His lung collapsed and stopped his heart," or "This is the beginning of his decline," or "He was *so* young." What have you said and who wants to hear it?

"Oh, your life is not so awful," a woman at my office told me. She once lived in India and knew whereof she spoke. At Samuel's funeral, a priest told me, "I don't envy you boys. This is your enterprise now, your vocation." He kissed me, as if sex between us was an option he held, then rode to the altar on a billow of white to a solitary place setting meant to serve us all.

Enzo's temperature remained the same through the night. I poured myself a drink—though I did not need it—to push myself over the edge of feeling. I took it down to the beach. There were still a few bright stars in the sky. Everything was shaded in rose, including the waves and the footprints in the sand, deceiving me and the men coming home from dancing into anticipating a beautiful day.

Since the deaths began, the certified social workers have quoted Shakespeare at us: "Give sorrow words." But the words we used now reek of old air in churches, taste of the dust that has gathered in the crevices of the Nativity and the Passion. Our condolences are arid as leaves. We are actors who have over-rehearsed our lines. When I left the Island one beautiful weekend, Noah asked, "Were you so close to this man you have to go to his funeral?" I told myself all the way to Philadelphia that I did not have to justify my mourning. One is responsible for feeling something and being done with it.

Give sorrow occasion and let it go, or your heart will imprison you in constant February, a chain-link fence around frozen soil, where your dead will stack in towers past the point of grieving. *Let your tears fall for the dead, and as one who is suffering begin the lament . . . do not neglect his burial.* Think of him, the one you loved, on his knees, on his elbows, his face turned up to look back in yours, his mouth dark in his dark beard. He was smiling because of you. You tied a silky rope around his wrists, then down around the base of his cock and balls, his anus raised for you. When you put your mouth against it, you ceased to exist. All else fell away. You had brought him, and he you, to that point where you are most your mind and most your body. His prostate pulsed against your fingers like a heart in a cave, *mind, body, body, mind,* over and over. Looking down at him, he who is dead and gone, then lying across the broken bridge of his spine, the beachhead of his back, you would gladly change places with him. *Let your weeping be bitter and your wailing fervent; then be comforted for your sorrow.* Find in grief the abandon you used to find in love; grieve the way you used to fuck.

Perry was out on the deck when I got back. He was naked and had covered himself with one hand when he heard steps on our boardwalk. With the other hand, he was hosing down the bathroom rugs on which Enzo had been sick. I could tell by the way he smiled at me that my eyes must have been red and swollen.

"There's been an accident," he said.

"I was a witness. Do you need help?"

"I've got it," he said, and waddled back inside for a bucket and disinfectant to do the bathroom floors.

Enzo opened the curtains on his room. I asked him how he was feeling.

"My fever's down a little. And my back hurts."

Stark asked him, "Do you think you can stay out here a couple of days and rest? Or do you want to go into the hospital?"

"You can fly in and be there in a half an hour," I said.

"One of us will go in with you," Stark said.

"I'm not sure. I think so," Enzo said, incapable of making a decision.

"What if I call your doctor and see what he says?" I asked.

The doctor's service answered and I left as urgent a message as I could. I began breaking eggs into a bowl, adding cinnamon and almond concentrate. The doctor's assistant called me back before the yolks and egg whites were beaten together. "What are the symptoms?" he asked.

"Fever, diarrhea."

"Back pain?"

"Yes."

"Is his breathing irregular?" the assistant asked.

"His breathing is irregular, his temperature is irregular, his pulse is irregular, and his bowel movement is irregular. My bet is he's dehydrated. What else do you need to know?"

"Has he been diagnosed with AIDS yet?"

"No," I said, "but he had his spleen removed two years ago. And Dr. Williams knows his medical history."

"I'll call you back," he said.

"How is he?" asked Noah. It was early for him to be out of bed. I began to suspect that no one had slept well.

"He's weak and now his back hurts. I think he'd like to go to the hospital."

"It's Sunday. They aren't going to do anything for him. All they'll do is admit him. He might as well stay here and I'll drive him in tomorrow."

Horst came out of Enzo's room. "That's not true. They can test oxygen levels in his blood for PCP and start treatment right away. And the sooner they catch these things, the easier they are to treat."

Horst had said what none of us would say—PCP—for if

it was *Pneumocystis carinii* pneumonia, then Enzo did have
AIDS. One more person in the house would have it, one more
to make it impossible to escape for a weekend, one more to
remind us of how short our lives were becoming.

The phone rang. Dr. Williams's assistant told me to get
Enzo in right away. "Get yourself ready," I said. "Your doctor
will be coming in just to see you. I'll call the airline to get you
a seat on the seaplane."

"Okay," Enzo said, relieved to have the decision made for
him. He put his feet on the floor and got his bearings. Stark
helped him fill a bag. Then I looked outside and saw what
appeared to be a sheet unfurling over the trees. Fog was coming
through the brambles the way smoke unwraps from a cigarette
and lingers in the heat of a lamp.

"Oh, my God, will you look at that," Joe said. "Another
lousy beach day. This has been the worst summer."

Perry called the Island airline. All flights were canceled
for the rest of the morning. Visibility of three miles was needed
for flight to the Island, and we couldn't even see beyond our
deck. Even voices from the neighboring houses sounded muf-
fled and far away for the first time all summer.

"We're going to have to find someone who will drive him
in," Perry said. "Unless he thinks he can handle the train."

"He's too sick for the train," I said.

"Who do we know with a car?" Perry asked. Joe took
Jules out for a walk. Noah went behind the counter, where
the batter for French toast was waiting. He began slicing chal-
lah and dipping it into batter, though no one was ready to
eat.

Perry said, "I wonder if Frank is driving back today."

"Call him," I said.

But Perry didn't get the response he expected. We heard
him say, "Frank, he's very sick. His doctor said to get him in
right away." He turned to us. "Frank says he'll drive Enzo in
if the fog doesn't clear up."

"Well, I can understand why he would feel put upon,"
Noah said. "I wouldn't want to give up my weekend, either."

At that point, I said, "I'm going in with Enzo."

Noah said, "He can go into the emergency room by himself. He doesn't need anyone with him." I said nothing but I did not turn away from him either. Perry looked at me and then to Noah. His lower lip dropped from under his mustache. Noah said, "Well, doesn't he have someone who could meet him there?"

"Enzo," I called, "is there anyone who could meet you in the city?"

"I guess I could call my friend Jim," he said.

"See," Noah said.

"Jim's straight," I said, not that I thought it really made any difference, but it sounded as if it did. We did, supposedly, know the ropes of this disease. "Enzo, who would you rather have with you, me or Jim?"

"You."

Noah raised his eyebrows and shrugged one shoulder. "I don't know why you feel you have to go into the emergency room."

"Because I am beginning to see what it will be like to be sick with this thing and not have anyone bring me milk or medication because it isn't convenient or amusing any longer."

Noah said, "I have been working at the Gay Men's Health Crisis for the past six years. I was one of the first volunteers."

"Oh, good, the institutional response. That reassures me," I said. Starting into my room to pack a bag, I bumped into Nils, who was coming out of the shower and didn't have any clothes on, not even a towel. Although Nils walked the beach in a bikini brief that left nothing to—nor satisfied—the imagination, he quickly covered himself and pressed his body against the wall to let me pass.

"I'm sorry if I kept you up last night," he said to me.

"It wasn't you. I was worried about Enzo," I said.

By eleven-thirty the fog was packed in as tight as cotton in a new jar of aspirin. Our friend with the car decided that since it was not a beach day, he could be doing things in the city. We were to meet him at the dock for the twelve o'clock ferry. He could not, however, take me as well, for he had promised two guests a ride and only had room for four in his jaunty little car.

Enzo and Perry seemed embarrassed by this. "I don't mind taking the train," I said. "I'll be able to read the Sunday *Times*."

Nils put his arm around me and walked me to the door. "I'll be gone when you come back. I'd like to leave you my address." I wanted to say a house gift would be more appropriate, something for the kitchen or a flowering plant. "It's unlikely that I'll ever get that far north," I said, "but thanks all the same. Maybe I'll drop you a line." The last thing I saw as I was leaving was his large head down over his plate, his arms on the table, a fork in a fist. He was a huge and odd-looking man. Stark said he had a face like the back of a bus, but it was actually worse than that. Nils was also the author of two books, working on a third about the Nazi occupation of Oslo. I saw the others join him around the table. He was probably ten times smarter than anyone there. Sharp words and arguments often defined the boundaries of personalities in this house, but Nils did not touch any of our borders. He simply did not fit in. And though tourists are insufferable after a point, I knew I should ask his forgiveness for my sin of inhospitality, but I couldn't make the overture to deserve it.

On the ferry, Enzo said, "I'm glad you're coming."

"I wanted out of that house," I said.

"I know."

We listened to our tape players so as not to speak about what was on our minds. People wore white sweaters and yellow mackintoshes. They held dogs in their laps, or the Sports section, or a beach towel in a straw purse; a man had his arm around his lover's shoulder, his fingertips alighted on the other's collarbone. No one spoke. It didn't seem to matter that the weekend was spoiled. We were safe in this thoughtless fog. The bay we crossed was shallow; it could hide neither monsters from the deep nor German submarines. It seemed all we needed to worry about was worrying too much; what we had to fear was often small and could be ignored. But as we entered the harbor on the other side, a dockworker in a small motorboat passed our ferry and shouted, "AIDS!" And in case we hadn't heard him, shouted again, "AIDS, AIDS!"

A man slid back the window and shouted back, "Crib death!" Then he slunk in his seat, ashamed of himself.

I read the paper on the train. I listened to Elgar, Bach, Barber, and Fauré. An adagio rose to its most poignant bar; the soprano sang the Pie Jesù with a note of anger, impatient that we should have to wait so long for everlasting peace, or that the price was so high, or that we should have to ask at all. I filled the empty time between one place and another with a moderate and circumspect sorrow delineated by the beginning, middle, and end of these adagios. Catharsis is not a release of emotion, it is a feast. Feel this. Take that. And you say, Yes, sir, thank you, sir. Something hardens above the eyes and your throat knots and you feel your self back into being. Friends die and I think, Good, that's over, let go of these intolerable emotions, life goes on. The train ride passed; I finished mourning another one. The train ride was not as bad as people say it is.

And Enzo had only arrived at the hospital ten minutes before me. The nurses at the emergency desk said I couldn't see him.

"I'm his care partner from the Gay Men's Health Crisis," I said, telling them more than they were prepared to hear. "Can I just let him know I'm here?" The lie worked as I was told it would.

Dr. Williams was there as well, standing over Enzo's gurney, which was in the middle of the corridor. "Was there any diarrhea?" he asked. Enzo said no, I said yes. "Fever?" "Over a hundred and five." "Did you have a productive cough?" he asked, and Enzo smiled. He pounded on the small of Enzo's back. "Does that hurt?" It did. The doctor was certain that Enzo's infection was one to which people who have had their spleens removed are vulnerable. We were moved to a little curtained room in the emergency ward.

"I'm not convinced it isn't PCP," Enzo said to me.

"Neither am I," said the attending physician, who had been outside the curtain with Enzo's chart. "Dr. Williams's diagnosis seems too logical. I want to take some tests just to make sure."

He asked for Enzo's health history: chronic hepatitis; idiopathic thrombocytopenia purpura; the splenectomy; herpes. Enzo sounded as if he were singing a tenor aria from *L'Elisir d'Amore*. The attending physician leaned over him, listened for the high notes, and touched him more like a lover than a doctor.

"You don't have to stay," Enzo said to me.

"I want to see if he comes back," I said.

"He reminds you of Samuel."

"A little bit."

"Do you think he's gay?"

"I don't think he'd be interested in me even if he was. Maybe you, though," I said.

Enzo smiled at that and fell asleep. The afternoon passed with nurses coming in to take more blood. He was wheeled out twice for X rays. A thermos of juice had broken in his overnight bag. I rinsed his sodden clothes and wrapped them in newspaper to take back to the house to wash. But his book about eating in Paris was ruined. He had been studying all summer for his trip to France the coming fall. Restaurants were highlighted in yellow, like passages in an undergraduate's philosophy book; particular dishes were starred.

He woke and saw me with it. "My shrink told me that we couldn't live our lives as if we were going to die of AIDS. I've been putting off this vacation for years," he said. "If there's anything you want to do, Clark, do it now."

"Do you want me to call anyone?" I asked.

"Have you called the house yet?"

"I thought I'd wait until we had something to tell them."

"Okay," he said, and went back to sleep. I read what I hadn't thrown away of the *Times*. In the magazine was an article titled "She Took the Test." I began to read it but skipped past the yeasty self-examination to get to the results. Her test had come back negative. I wondered whether she would have written the piece had it come back positive.

Enzo woke and asked again, "Have you called the house yet?"

"No, I was waiting until we knew something certain."

"If I had PCP, you would tell them right away," he said.

"Yes, Enzo, but we don't know that yet," I said, but he had already fallen back to sleep. He hadn't had anything to eat all day, and hadn't been given anything to reduce the fever. Because he was dehydrated, they had him on intravenous, but he seemed to be sweating as quickly as the fluid could go into his body. I felt the accusation anyway, and it was just. I had not called the house precisely because they were waiting for me to call and because I was angry at them.

It was eight o'clock that evening before the handsome doctor returned again. "There is too much oxygen in your blood for it to be PCP," he told us. "But we found traces of a bacterial pneumonia, the kind of infection Dr. Williams was referring to. Losing your spleen will open you up to these kinds of things, and there's no prevention. We'll put you on intravenous penicillin for a week and you'll be fine."

Enzo grinned. He would not have to cancel his trip to Paris. His life and all the things he had promised himself were still available to him. An orderly wheeled him to his room, and I followed behind with his bag. It was not AIDS, but it would be someday, a year from now, maybe, two, unless science or the mind found prophylaxis. He knew this as well as I did. Not this year, he said, but surely within five. No one knows how this virus will affect us over the years, what its impact will be on us when we are older, ten years after infection, fifteen—fifteen years from now? When I was eleven years old, I never thought I would live to be twenty-six, which I thought to be the charmed and perfect age. I think fifteen years from now, and I come to fifty. How utterly impossible that seems to me, how unattainable. I have not believed that I would live to the age of forty for two years now.

"You'll call the house now," he said as I was leaving.

"Yes."

"I appreciate your being here."

I turned in the doorway. Several responses came to mind—that I hadn't really done so much, that anybody would have done what I had done. Enzo saw me thinking, however, and smiled to see me paused in thought. "I wanted to say that reality compels us to do the right thing if we live in the real world," I said. "But that's not necessarily true, is it?"

"It can put up a compelling argument," Enzo said. "Don't be mad at Noah. I didn't expect him to drive me in."

With Enzo in his room, the penicillin going into his veins, feeling better simply at the idea of being treated, I submitted to my own exhaustion and hunger. I went home and collected a week's worth of mail from a neighbor. There was nothing to eat in the refrigerator, but on the door was a review from the *Times* of a restaurant that had just opened in the neighborhood and that I had yet to try. The light was flashing on my answering machine, but I could not turn it on, knowing the messages would be from my housemates. I called the man who drove Enzo in to tell him how much suffering he had saved Enzo from, exaggerating for the answering machine, which I was glad had answered for him. I turned my own off so that I couldn't receive any more messages and left my apartment with the mail I wanted to read.

Walking down a dark street of parking garages to the restaurant that had been reviewed, I saw a gold coin-shaped wrapper—the kind that chocolate dollars and condoms come in—embedded in the hot asphalt. Pop caps glittered in the street like an uncorked galaxy stuck in the tar.

Horst's prediction came true. While Horst was dying two years later, Perry was at an AIDS conference with his new little boyfriend. When confronted, he'd say, "Horst wanted me to go." Perry would include Horst's death notice with fundraising appeals for the gay youth organization he volunteered for. Everyone who knows him learns to expect the worst from

him. And Enzo would be right, also. A year or so later, he
was diagnosed with KS, then with lymphoma.

The *Times* would eventually report more on the subject
and still get things wrong. Not journalism as the first draft of
history, but a rough draft, awkward and splintered and rude
and premeditated. They will do a cover story on the decimation
of talent in the fashion industry and never once mention that
the designers, stylists, illustrators, show room assistants,
makeup artists, or hairdressers were gay. How does one write
about a battle and not give name to the dead, even if they are
your enemy?

The dead were marching into our lives like an occupying
army. Noah's defenses were weakening, but the illness did not
threaten him personally. He was sero-negative and would stay
that way. Even so, he had found himself in a standstill of pain,
a silo of grief, which I myself had not entered, though I knew
its door well. Perry thought of Samuel every time he saw me,
and, in turn, probably thought of Horst. I suspected he saw
his new boyfriend as a vaccine against loneliness and not as an
indication that he had given up hope. We had found ourselves
in an unacceptable world. And an unacceptable world can com-
pel unacceptable behavior.

But that night, I turned around without my supper and went
back home to listen to my messages. The first was from Horst,
who would have been put up to call because he was the closest
to me and the closest to death. "Clark, are you there? It's
Horst," he said, as if I wouldn't have recognized his accent.
"We want to know how Enzolina is. Please call. We love you."

For a long stretch of tape, there was only the sound of
breathing, the click of the phone, over and over again. Perry's
voice came next.

"I was very touched by your going into the hospital today
and how you took care of Enzo last night. I want to tell you
that now," he said, in a low voice. "I hope you understand
that there was nothing to be done last night, and you were

doing it. Sometimes I don't think Horst understands that the nights he is almost comatose that I am suffering beside him, fully conscious. I saw your face when Noah did not offer to drive Enzo in. I thought perhaps it was because they can't take the dog on the train, or because he had taken tomorrow off to spend with Joe. But I can't make any excuses for him. You are so morally strict sometimes, like an unforgiving mirror. Oh, let's see . . . Horst is feeling much better. Call us please."

Then Stark called to find out whether either Enzo or I needed anything, and told me when he would be home if I wanted to call. And then Joe. "Where are you, Clark? Oh, God, you should have seen Noah go berserk today when he took the garbage out and found maggots in the trash cans. He screamed, 'I can't live like this the rest of the summer.' He's been cleaning windows and rolling up rugs. She's been a real mess all day. Oh, God, now he's sweeping under the bed. I can't decide if I should calm him down or stay out of his way. The house should look nice when you get back."

Finally Noah called. "Clark, where are you, Superman? I have to tell you something. You know the novel you lent me to read? I accidentally threw it in the washing machine with my bedclothes. Please call."

My lover, Samuel, used to tell a story about himself. It was when he was first working with the Theater of the Deaf. The company had been improvising a new piece from an outline that Samuel had devised, when he said something that provoked a headstrong and violent young actor, deaf since birth. "I understand you," Samuel said in sign, attempting to silence him, if that's the word. The young actor's eyes became as wild as a horse caught in a burning barn; his arms flew this way and that, as if furious at his own imprecision. Samuel needed an interpreter. "You do not understand this," the actor was saying, pointing to his ears. "You will never understand."

You let go of people, the living and the dead, and return to your self, to your own resources, like a widower, a tourist alone in a foreign country. Your own senses become important, and other people's sensibilities a kind of Novocaine, blocking out your own perceptions, your ability to discriminate, your taste. There is something beyond understanding, and I do not know what it is, but as I carried the phone with me to the couch, a feeling of generosity came over me, of creature comforts having been satisfied well and in abundance, like more than enough to eat and an extra hour of sleep in the morning. Though I hadn't had either, I was in a position to anticipate them both. The time being seeps in through the senses: the plush of a green sofa; the music we listen to when we attempt to forgive ourselves our excesses; the crazing pattern on the ginger jar that reminds us of why we bought it in the first place, not to mention the shape it holds, the blessing of smells it releases. The stretch of time and the vortex that it spins around, thinning and thickening like taffy, holds these pleasures, these grace notes, these connections to others, to what it is humanly possible to do.

SUCCOR

—

It was said that the reason Italian pilots flew so close to the ground was to follow the roads, but Kerch Slattery thought they might just be taking in the view. His plane circled Rome awaiting a ground crew's impromptu strike—*un sciopero*—which could last days or just the length of a coffee break. Fortunately, he had a window seat. The flight around Rome reminded him of Manhattan's Circle Line cruise; once around the island, you've seen the town, and you can go back to Joliet without another thought, the victor, the survivor, triumphant, alive. If Kerch had been handed a microphone, he could have identified sights out the window for the other passengers. It was fifteen years since he last had been in Rome, but he knew all the domes: St. Peter's was easy, and S. Andrea della Valle, but there was S. Ivo's, S. Eustachio, and the handsome and humble square dome on the synagogue. He knew the streets and piazzas as well: the Via Arenula, Via del Corso, the Campidoglio, Piazza Navonna; that way was the S. Luigi dei Francesi with its three Caravaggios; around the corner was S. Agostino's, which only had one, the Madonna of the Pilgrims (to look at her one imagines the model was a streetwalker), but that served as an interesting contrast to the classical Junoesque sculpture of the Madonna by Sansovino, covered with jewel votive offerings, as ancient statues of goddesses often were. "To see her surrounded by blazing candles and to watch her devotees touch the foot that has been worn smooth by the millions [necessitating, Kerch recalled, a silver prosthesis] who have gone before is to realize that the cult of the mother strikes some deep atavistic chord in the Roman mind" is how his guidebook mildly put it. Did the real idea of mother fall somewhere between the two images, Kerch asked himself, or was there really that much of a difference between a goddess you paid for favors or the voluptuous one who held you in her arms as if you, not she, were the object of worship? But that thought was replaced quickly by another one: I've been here before.

"Go back," Father Casey had said to him, and left a small amount of money after his death for Kerch to do so. "The city won't have changed, but you'll have." Casey implied that as he himself was dying of AIDS, Kerch, by virtue of being seropositive for the virus, would become ill, also. It was just a matter of time.

The thought came back, or actually, the thought progressed, as he stood beneath the Bernini angel (there was actually some doubt about that, as he recalled) on the Ponte S. Angelo. The angel was covered with scaffolding and straw matting; a sign claimed that a major corporation was paying for the restoration; he couldn't see which instrument of the Passion this angel held. The restorer, wearing white overalls like an American house painter, opened a door into the scaffolding, then closed it behind himself. Kerch opened it again, and the restorer said, *"Buon giorno."* He looked up.

It was the angel with the nail. The head of the nail was rounded and sloped, rather like a mushroom, but more like something else, Kerch observed. The smile on the angel was not without its own knowledge of the private joke. That is when Kerch thought, Perhaps I should have gone someplace else.

Henry James had said that Rome can increase tenfold one's liability toward misery, and his first time here, as a melancholic nineteen-year-old, Kerch had indeed been miserable. Either James was right or the city was just obliging; misery loves company, or at least a good mirror. The city's moods and one's own tended to be concomitant, or maybe there was just a lag time on the city's part, like someone who will go for a walk with you if given enough time to comb her hair.

"To love and have my love returned was my heart's desire, and it would be all the sweeter if I could also enjoy the body of the one who loved me." St. Augustine's *Confessions*. Well, that was the crux of it, right there, the real reason Kerch had been miserable in Rome, young and gay, and in a strange town where every man was more handsome than the last.

Dr. Palermo, the psychiatrist he had gone to only once, surmised as much himself, believing as he did that time spent celibate was a sad waste of time, and arranged for a meeting between his own son, Niccolo, who had a passion for American poetry, and Kerch, a literature major at an American school that had a campus in Rome. "How do you say this word?" Niccolo asked, pointing to his Whitman.

"Athwart," Kerch said.

"A–thwart," Niccolo attempted, the English *th* as difficult for him as the Italian rolled *r* or the *gli* sound was for Kerch. "Read the line to me," Niccolo demanded.

Kerch read as Niccolo nervously pounded his fingers on the tabletop, and his heart raced to catch up with their quickening beat. " 'You settled your head athwart my hips and gently turned over upon me, and parted the shirt from my bosombone, and plunged your tongue to my barestript heart, and reached till you felt my beard, and reached till you held my feet.' "

Where he now stood on the Ponte San'Angelo, Kerch could see the shuttered window that overlooked the Tiber where he and his psychiatrist's son had made love in the cloudy light of a February afternoon. Dr. Palermo sent him a bill for his single consultation.

They had never become lovers, though they continued to have sex three or four times a week. Sex was possible, a relationship prohibited. It had been a matter of class, almost illegal in an ancient Roman sense, Niccolo a patrician, Kerch a plebe. But they had become companions. On the back of Niccolo's Vespa, Niccolo maneuvering the streets of Rome, Kerch would sing, "Whenever blues becomes my only song, I concentrate on you."

Promiscuous (adj.), consisting of diverse things or members: miscellaneous, indiscriminate, mixed, motley, multifarious. Lacking a definite plan, purpose, or pattern: random, desultory, haphazard, irregular, spot.

"You've brought dying people into your home," the magazine writer said to him, "people who had no place else to go. Why do you do it?"

"I have a spare room," Kerch said.

The spare room overlooked a sliver of a park at the top of West End Avenue. A motley assortment of men—he had been indiscriminate in whom he let in—had died in the room, looking down at the statue in the park built in memory of Ida and Isidore Strauss, who had gone down in the *Titanic*. When he had moved into the rent-stabilized apartment as a graduate student, he thought the Strausses were sisters; to himself, he called the statue *Remembrance*. She lay across the top of a granite wall, reclining on one arm, the fingers of one hand loose across her lips. From a distance, she looked as if she might be smiling. Up close, one saw her sad hooded eyes contemplating an empty basin and dried pool, as if she were reading Eliot, "Dry the pool, dry concrete, brown edged . . . human kind/Cannot bear very much reality."

The apartment was filled with medical apparatus; sometimes it looked like an infirmary; I.V. poles, sturdy plastic containers for medical waste, a kitchen cabinet devoted to medications—some effective, most useless. The police came each time someone died in his apartment, as was the law. They always knew that AIDS was the cause of death. Kerch once overheard one of the cops say, "This place is like a Roach Motel. They check in and they don't check out." The comment didn't bother him; he had had the same thought himself, as did the men who came there and died.

He used to be a buddy, but that was when people volunteered out of a sense of identification with the sick. That time seemed to have passed. The volunteers who helped the sick were still called buddies, but the people who were sick were called clients.

"My client doesn't think he needs me, but he will, he will," Kerch heard a man say as he wandered through the last party for volunteers.

"You really have to tell them what your limits are," another said. "Otherwise, they expect you to drop everything and come running over just because they're lonely."

"I understand that Terry has been in the hospital for six months, but all he does is gossip about the doctors and the nurses, and it's boring. Maybe I should speak to him about that."

"My client hemorrhaged last week."

"Mine died; I'm waiting to be assigned another," said a woman.

"You're really wonderful to be doing this," someone told

her. She smiled, then looked sad and then neutral, a Juno among the volunteers.

Kerch wondered whether the buddies would speak with more humility if they were called succors instead.

Father Casey's remains had been the last to be carried from the spare room. Kerch had tried to talk Casey out of leaving the hospital when it was obvious that doctors could do nothing more for him. "If you start coughing and you can't stop, I won't know what to do for you," Kerch said. "If you're in pain, I'll be helpless."

"I'm not afraid of that, if you aren't," Casey said.

Casey had been living in a Catholic community in upstate New York when he was diagnosed, and came to Manhattan for better medical care. The Jesuits had tossed him out for his homosexuality, but the Vatican wouldn't defrock him.

Kerch assumed that Casey was too close to death to suffer the rejection of his order, that he wasn't angry, because the dying so often let go of such things. But that wasn't the case. "No, I'm grateful to the Jesuits. They educated me, satisfied answers to old questions, and gave me moments of mystery and serenity. They helped me find an inner ground, the place of my being. I think that's where I'll go when I die," Casey told him. "You, on the other hand, secular humanist that you are, God only knows where you'll end up."

"Hell, then."

"No, the devil hates a liberal."

Kerch said, "So Hell is filled with Republicans."

"Yes." The priest smiled. "And they just love the place."

Kerch had been with him when Casey died, knew the moment. Whatever pain Casey had been in, he was not telling Kerch. Kerch had learned over and over again how little can be done for someone who was ill, even as hard as it was to know the contents of another's heart. With the sick, he was not outside looking in as their interior worlds were changed by drugs and viruses and bacteria; he was outside looking *at*

them, as if through a shop window, or at someone halluci-
nating. When Casey died, however, something happened that
had nothing to do with the body in the bed. It was as if the
inner garden he had spoken of simply overflowed into the
room. Casey was there, and was there for three days after
the remains—the remains to be seen—had been carried out.
And Kerch sat in the room, smoking cigarettes, drinking coffee
and wine, as if he was in a garden, or a park, or even the Piazza
S. Maria in Trastevere, watching the foot traffic pass, the light
change across the face of the church.

He feared that Casey's death, and the deaths before him, had
settled like sediment to the bottom of his heart, layer over
layer, like the level of civilizations here in the Eternal City.
    On the Ponte S. Angelo, he remembered a teacher, Fink,
an Austrian, a handsome man, who always wore one of two
turtleneck sweaters, black or gray cashmere. Maybe as much
as Niccolo, Fink had determined Kerch's impression of the
city. It was rumored—and probably not true—that he had
four doctorates. He taught everything, from Baroque architecture to the plays of Bertolt Brecht. Little he ever said in
class could be corroborated in texts or art history books. Kerch
could remember a class huddled in a fine fog, Fink, his gray
hair shiny with jewel-like mist, pointing to the elongated fig-
ures of the angels, saying that they were designed to give the
impression of fluidity and movement to passengers in carriages
going over the bridge. "Your own speed and motion gives
them flight," Fink said. Since then, Fink and his young son
had been killed in a car crash on the coast of Spain. His wife,
back in Austria, sent money for the bodies to be buried there.
    There was a current trend for the dying young to request
that there be no funeral, no wake, just a memorial service a
month or two after their deaths. The fashion did not consider
the needs of the living; it did not help their bereavement process. It was being forced to feel loss long after mourning had
become memory. Even two months after a death, time had

tempered grief to some extent; death had been accepted, the
dead gone for good. If one was not exactly over it, you were
past the public display of sadness. For a while, friends and
associates joked that they only saw one another at memorial
services. Eventually, Kerch observed that people merely nodded to him, and he to them, from across the room, and then
rushed for the door afterward, like operagoers who rush out
during ovations to get to parked cars, dinner reservations, the
baby-sitter back home.

One who died in his apartment requested that there be
no funeral for him, so Kerch looked at the death notices in
the newspaper and found a funeral in the neighborhood with
the casual interest of one looking for a movie. Then he put on
a dark jacket, a white shirt. He signed the registration book
and was handed a program. He was ready to sit with strangers
and have a good cry. As he looked around the church, however,
he found that he recognized a good many mourners.

Kerch opened the program. A snapshot had been inserted
of the deceased, a fortyish man with a sexy bald head and sexier
overlapped front teeth. "What luck," Kerch said to himself, "I
knew this one."

A woman was moving up the aisle of the church from
one pew to another. People were looking at her, horrified. She
sat down next to Kerch and said, "I didn't know the dead, but
I offer my condolences. Were the two of you close?"

Kerch considered her a moment, then said, "We met at a
j.o. party."

After a pause the woman said, "What a coincidence. I
love Jo Stafford. I always have. And the two of you so
young."

During the service, friends of the deceased read a poem
by Edna St. Vincent Millay, "Dirge Without Music," senti-
mental but appropriately touching, and someone else read from
"Little Gidding." Kerch was in his element, although he saved
his enthusiasm for the hymns, "Jerusalem, My Happy Home"
and "Amazing Grace," for he had been frustrated out of familiar

expressions of grief at a succession of Jewish funerals. (He knew the Jews at this service—they were the ones trying to look up the hymns in *The Book of Common Prayer*.)

When he got back home, the victim's family was attempting to move everything that belonged to Kerch out of his own apartment. The police were called and stopped them.

"Money," the family said. "Wasn't there any money? We sent him five hundred dollars."

"He was here six months," Kerch said. "What do you think that went for?"

Kerch saw the mother look around the room, for a picture or a shirt, anything so as not to leave empty-handed. He pulled off the watch he had gotten as a confirmation present when he was eleven; he pulled off a ring he had bought in Rome. "He gave these to me," Kerch said. "But he had a fever; he was probably delirious. I'm sure he meant for you to have them."

She tried the ring on, and began to weep. She held the watch up to her cheek, and turned it over in her hand. On the back of the watch, she read Kerch's name, including the one he had chosen for himself, the date April 11, 1966, the words *God's love*. She handed them back to him.

"Sebastian must be your confirmation name. I bet the nuns helped you pick it out," she said. "He was the patron saint of plagues."

"I thought he was the patron saint of cowboys."

Her face collapsed. "My son would have said something like that, too," she said. "He left me nothing, then. No keepsakes. Nothing to take home with me."

"We'll find something," Kerch said, and took her into the spare room.

"A scrapbook," she said when he pulled out the album that was stuck between the bed and the wall.

Kerch had never seen it before, either. "No, it's a commonplace book," he said. It was filled with passages from books and magazine articles, and illustrated with postcards the man had found in museum gift shops. It was definitely the commonplace book of a sick man, the passages that filled it colored by months spent ill in this room. Kerch recognized almost all the excerpts, like the one from Whitman's *Specimen Days*. "The dead, the dead, the dead—*our* dead—ours all (all, all, all, finally dear to me) . . . our young men once so handsome and so joyous, taken from us, the son from the mother, the husband from the wife, the dear friend from the dear friend." Then Kerch recognized his own handwriting along the margin of a poem torn out of *The Collected Poems of Emily Dickinson*. The source of the commonplace book were the books from his own shelves.

" 'There is a pain—so utter—It swallows substance up,' " the man's mother read, pausing at the dashes. She read formally and well, as if she was reading from the Bible to a Sunday school class. "This must have given him so much comfort in his final days," she said.

"Well, it certainly kept him busy," Kerch said.

"Thank you for finding this," she said. "To know what he was thinking all these months, I'll feel as if I had been with him."

On top of the Castel Sant'Angelo was the archangel Michael brandishing his sword. Kerch opened *The Companion Guide to Rome,* which had been the guidebook of choice for something like twenty years, and read, "In 590 . . . the first year of Gregory the Great's reign, Rome was decimated by plague and the pope ordered forty processions to make their way through the city to intercede for God's help. People fell out of the ranks, dying by the wayside, as men and women, priests and children, marched through the empty streets. Just as Gregory was about to enter St. Peter's, he saw a vision of the Archangel Michael, on the summit of what was left of Hadrian's tomb, sheathing his sword. The pestilence ceased. . . ."

"Yeah, sure," Kerch said. Once, his Catholic-taught mind would not have questioned the miracle. Even after he stopped believing, he went on to believe that there must have been an historical fact to explain the miracle, a coincidence. Across town was a portrait of the Madonna, supposedly hand-delivered by two angels to Pope John in the year 523. In two other epidemics, 590 and 1656, the image was carried through the streets in a penitential procession, and wherever the Madonna passed, the pestilence or plague was said to cease. It would not have occurred to him before, nor to the Church, which had its own explanation for illness, that whatever the cause of the pestilence, virus or bacteria, it had simply killed who it could kill.

He had a casual acquaintance with a man in his own neighborhood, someone he did not even know was ill until they met by chance one morning in a coffeehouse across from Strauss Park. On any other occasion, Kerch probably would have said hello and sat at another table, but the sight of the man's face, the loss of weight, the color of his complexion, but especially the lesion that had turned the white of one eye deep red, had the effect of sudden confession, sudden intimacy, as if in truth they shared an accomplished past, a war, an addiction, a struggle, in common.

"The weather has been marvelous, hasn't it?" Dennis said, almost as if he had something to do with it.

And Kerch said it had, as if to give him credit for it. It had indeed been a beautiful Indian summer, a reprieve after October's tongue lashings and premature snow. The leaves on the ginkgo trees in Strauss Park, always the last to fall, were lemon; the air bright as seltzer. An old Chinese couple were picking up the fecund ginkgo berries off the ground.

"You recall the weather two weeks ago, the snow?" Dennis asked.

"Wednesday."

"I really thought I was dying that night," Dennis said. "I went to sleep not expecting to wake up."

"Well, you look pretty good."

"I healed myself," he said to Kerch.

"Why, that's terrific," Kerch said, wishing that he had sat at another table. "I'm very happy for you."

"Oh, I can see you looking at my lesions," Dennis said, "but they are disappearing; I know they are."

"No, I'm glad for you," Kerch said, and squeezed the man's hand. Who was he to doubt, to question?

"I called my father, whom I haven't spoken to in six years. We're going to spend Thanksgiving together," Dennis said. He looked out the window and said after a moment, "Really, I have no idea why anyone would call AIDS into his life."

"Yes, well, you know."

This had been a man, Kerch knew, who used to read newspaper articles all the way to the end, hungry for the world. He had stopped reading papers, however, because the bad news interfered with his state of grace, his positive attitude. Kerch thought that this must explain why men in other times went into monasteries, to close out a world beyond their control, protected by the monastery walls, and from their own thoughts by a theology that rationalized chaos. It did not occur to him that this was much the same reason he brought homeless people with AIDS into his own home.

"Do you have anyone staying with you now?" Dennis asked. It was well known that Kerch brought people into his home.

"Yes, he's not doing so well."

"If your friend is sick, it is because he wants to be sick," Dennis said.

"But, darling," Kerch said. "Don't we both know people who died even though they wanted to live?"

"They accepted a different reality," Dennis said.

Shortly, after Thanksgiving though, they ran into one another again. The weather had turned bad; the fleshy ginkgo berries were squashed against the gray cobblestone in Strauss Park. By this time, the KS had overwhelmed Dennis's face. He had lost another twenty pounds; his clothes hung off of him as if they were borrowed from a larger man. Dennis looked away from Kerch, and wouldn't speak to him, as if embarrassed, as if defeated. A few months later, he died.

Kerch stepped off the Ponte S'Angelo and walked down the Via dei Coronari, the street of the rosary makers, who once sold their wares to poor pilgrims on their way to St. Peter's. No rosaries now, but antique shops whose wares were beyond the reach of any but the very rich. A shopkeeper once told Kerch he could always come back to look at something he couldn't afford to buy. "It's enough to know that beautiful things exist," she said.

Kerch turned down the Via della Pace and into the piazza of the same name. The day, the piazza, and the church were the color of tarnished silver. Fink used to give a three-hour morning lecture beneath the ceiling fresco at the Il Gesù for his seminar in Art and Ideas, and then they would come here and look at the facade of the S. Maria della Pace. Of course, the ideas were generally his own; if a student said something he disagreed with, Fink would shout, *"Ma che stronzo."* His lecture beneath the ceiling fresco was on persuasive splendor ("the very opposite of Brecht's alienation effect"), the premise behind the opulent and exuberant theatrics of the Baroque church, that the riches of heaven could be previewed here on earth, or that the mystery of Christ's love did not need priestly mediators, as could be seen in the face of Bernini's St. Teresa, that, yes, someday all this would be yours, was yours now, did indeed exist.

What did we need to be persuaded of now? Kerch wondered. The world had gotten away from us. Did we now have a raw and chafing need for others to tell us that everything would be all right, perhaps, that the universe provides, and what it won't we needn't worry over? Did we just need someone to undress us and undress for us, touch our bodies gently, and put us to bed?

Fink's lecture had ended in front of the S. Maria della Pace. "The convex atrium, the concave wings give the illusion of taking up greater space than they actually do. The church itself is really quite small, but the multiplicity of details, including even the grain of the travertine, a stone common to the region and to Baroque masonry, focus the eye and extend our attention."

Kerch thought, What am I seeing, what am I seeing really?

There was his memory of the church, and there was the church itself right in front of him, and in that the whole of the church and the piazza seemed more articulated to him. It seemed that he was seeing them both at the same time, as if through an antique stereograph at twin photographs that were taken at slightly different angles (in his case, the angle of fifteen years, though time meant nothing in Rome) to give the impression of depth.

He stepped back to get another view of the church within the piazza designed for the traffic jam of horse-drawn carriages, when the church had become fashionable for its afternoon Mass. As he did so, several boys entered the piazza on their way home from school, kicking a ball among them. The ball hit the leg of an old woman who had come behind them, her hands full from shopping.

"*Prego, signora, me scusa,*" a little boy with dark, sad eyes said to her. He looked up at Kerch, his eyes now moist with faked mortification. "*Mi scusa, signore.*" The woman turned to Kerch, impressed herself by the boy's little act, and spoke as if she were a Renaissance courtesan: "They kick with their feet, not with their eyes."

He came into a piazza where Cellini boasted he had killed a rival jeweler. There had been a plague in Cellini's time as well, and it had been blamed on the conjunction of Jupiter and Mars. A man of the Church, at the time, Cardinal Gastaldi, said that anything the doctors wrote about the pestilence produced "Much smoke and little light." He said that medical remedies against the plague were no use and at times dangerous. The only remedy for it were pills made of three ingredients: *cito, longe,* and *tarde*—"run swiftly, go far, and return late." Doctors had to be compelled to tend the sick who were kept in lazarettos, or pesthouses.

In his confessions, Cellini wrote, "The epidemic disease continuing to rage for many months, I took to a freer course of life, because many of my acquaintances had died of it, while I remained in perfect health." He was twenty-three at the time, and eventually stricken himself, though he survived.

Kerch traversed the short length of the Via Giulia, then stopped to look back at it. So much had the city become a part of him when first he came here, he believed that a surgeon opening him up would not see viscera but this particular view. The street had once been envisioned as a major thoroughfare to the Vatican, the enclosed bridge just above his head was designed by Michelangelo and was to have gone clear across the river and to have connected two palaces. Now one of the few straight roads of the inner city, it seemed hardly more than a passionate alley. It did not seem to suffer, didn't demand attention, didn't even need a human being on its cobblestone to give it scale or purpose. It set out for a certain greatness and fell so far short of it, lasted and survived, that it could be smug in its established existence.

To his left was the Mascherone fountain, one of three huge, puzzling masks in the city that dated back to the ancient city. In a former life, it might have been a sewer cap; who knew? It, too, had been intended for greater things when it was placed in the wall; it was meant to have been fed by a major aqueduct that never made it quite this far. Water merely dribbled over its huge bottom lip now and made the face seem all the more human because of it, unblinking and insentient, someone who can only sigh and babble, drool and spit, because he knows more than he can make sense of. Or as Festus said to Saul, later Paul, "Much learning does make thee mad."

The S. Maria dell'Orazione e Morte just beyond the arch of Michelangelo's abbreviated bridge, according to his guidebook, belonged to an order whose purpose was to collect the bodies of the unknown dead and give them a Christian burial. A winged skeleton on the facade pointed to a scroll that read, "ME TODAY, YOU TOMORROW."

Kerch's doctor had called him about a month before he left for Rome with the results of his last blood tests, including a new test that allegedly measured viral activity. It was eleven o'clock on a Sunday night; Kerch was already asleep when the phone rang. Casey answered it and woke him up. Kerch and his doctor stayed on the phone for nearly an hour and a half.

"There doesn't seem to be active virus. Your T-4 cells are very low, but low T-4 cells is not incompatible with normal life," the doctor said. "You're more vulnerable now, but it doesn't mean that you will get an infection."

"If my viral activity is negligible," Kerch asked, "how do you explain this depletion of T-cells?"

"Attrition of the players."

"You can't tell by these dwindling numbers whether or not I'll go on to develop full-blown AIDS?"

"No, and if more people start taking AZT as an antiviral, or aerosol pentamidine as a pneumonia prophylaxis, we won't know; we'll never know. It all remains to be seen."

Kerch asked when he should start AZT. Everyone knew it was highly toxic, there was bone-marrow depletion, some muscle atrophy. It was feared to be a carcinogen that would invade every cell in the body. But the real reason that he was afraid to take the drug was that it would change the way he saw himself; it meant that there was something wrong with him; that if he didn't take it, he would probably become ill.

"There is no magic number," his doctor said. "If you decide to start taking it, I will support your decision. I am seeing other patients with higher counts than yours; they have lymphadenopathy, impetigo, anal herpes, fatigue, erosion of platelets . . . still normal, moving to abnormal."

"I could have been at that point years ago," Kerch said.

"We're all different . . . individual science."

Casey stood by listening to the whole conversation. When

Kerch hung up the phone, Casey placed a bottle of AZT in front of him. "What are you waiting for?" Casey asked. "Do you think that your T-cells are going to turn around and start going up on their own?"

"They don't mean anything," Kerch said. "I know someone who has had less than two hundred for five years, and no opportunistic infections."

"Don't forget, I was where you are now just eight months ago," Casey said. "You are afraid of identifying with me, and if you don't, you will end up like me, treading time in the darkness waiting for a cure."

"I don't know," Kerch said. "What if I can't handle it?"

"Soon there might be something else. You just have to be prepared to take it," Casey said. "It's too late for me, obviously, but it looks like the disease will become a manageable chronic condition."

"When? And what does that mean . . . manageable chronic condition? Manageable for whom? What's being managed?"

"There's hope."

"When?"

Casey backed off. He knew of Kerch's kitchen cabinet totally filled with useless chemicals and drugs that had neither prolonged a life, nor decreased the duration of an illness, nor saved anyone any pain. Each drug had been the harbinger of the end of the epidemic. They both had read an editorial in the newspaper that had waxed rhapsodic about a new drug, alleged evidence at how far science had progressed in combating the disease. Everyone was talking about it. Casey had tried to get into the trial and was told that he was too ill. Kerch was told that he was too healthy. And then the trial was canceled. The drug was totally forgotten and hope transferred to the next drug that showed promise in the test tube.

Casey asked, "Do you have any idea what you want to do with the rest of your life?"

"No, I don't even know how to plan for it. Do I live for the moment? And what is the moment? Is the moment basing

my hopes in a future that may not even exist? Do I tie my
puny savings up in long-term or short-term investments? Do
I go back to Rome, where I was happy once? Or someplace
I've never been before? The only thing I know anything about
anymore is AIDS. I know more about this epidemic than I
can recall of my college major. I've thought about going back
to school to get a degree in public health, but what if I get
sick after two years at Yale or Columbia, and I wasted all that
time? Or just as bad, what if they find a cure? Then what do
I do?"

"If you could have anything . . ."

Kerch said, "Sex with abandon."

He walked back out to the Tiber to the Ponte Sisto, which
crossed the Tiber like a spine of sun-bleached bone. On one
parapet, he saw something that took a moment for him to
translate. It was the Star of David surrounded by question
marks. The Jewish question. That was painted in red. Beneath
that was painted in black, HITLER WAS RIGHT. On the opposite
parapet was the inscription carved there when the bridge was
built: YOU WHO PASS BY HERE OFFER A PRAYER TO GOD SO
THAT SIXTUS IV, EXCELLENT PONTIFES MAXIMUS, MAY BE
HEALTHY AND FOR LONG SO PRESERVED. ANY OF YOU,
WHOEVER YOU ARE, TO WHOM THIS REQUEST IS MADE, BE
HEALTHY, TOO.

The people who used the word *hope* were usually unin-
fected and/or heterosexual, whose only source of information
about the epidemic was the mainstream media. And, of course,
none of these people were tending the sick. They confused
hope with certainty, the fait accompli. They grasped at the
simplest mechanical description of how some new drug would
theoretically work, and discussed it as if it had already eradicated the disease, as if they had been released from worrying
about it anymore. Their hope absolved them even of the ne-
cessity to be sympathetic. Fear of the new drug, let alone
skepticism, was not allowed into discussion.

It was not their hope that Kerch minded; like any particular faith, it was a private matter. He only wanted his friends to say outright that his fears were justified, and that they hoped he did not get sick, and that if he did get sick, they hoped that some new drug or drugs would work for him and have no toxic side effects, and that they would pay for that drug if he couldn't himself. And that they would be there for him if the drug did not work.

The chestnut trees were bare. The river swelled with mud. It was the warmest winter Rome had had in—twenty, thirty-five, fifty years, the century? Everyone told him a different story. He was now hurrying to meet Niccolo at the Sora Lella, a restaurant on the Tiberina, the little island in the middle of the river. There was a hospital on the island where Niccolo worked as a pathologist. A hospice had existed on that sight since the Middle Ages, and a religious order had founded this hospital on that site during the settecento.

At the Ponte Fabricio, Kerch stopped to look at the four-headed Janus, the Roman god who guarded over all beginnings. He opened *The Companion Guide to Rome,* which said, "The island has long been associated with the art of healing; a Temple of Aesculapius was built there after the great plague in 291 B.C. The temple was very large and constructed with porticoes where sick people could sleep the night in the hope that the god would visit them in their dreams and prescribe a cure."

Over the temple, a Christian church was built at the end of the tenth century, and people used to come with ex-votos, models of human arms and legs, in the hopes of, or with thanks for, cures. They brought tiny replicas of their arms and legs made in silver. He wondered what they had brought for other maladies—jewel-encrusted hearts, or tiny heads carved in ivory, flesh-colored silks for cancers, wooden dolls if it was a child sick? What, he wondered, could represent and heal his own immune system? A bottle of wine, a bucket of blood, his confirmation watch, the numbers and hands of which had long stopped glowing in the dark?

* * *

Casey was in the hospital for six weeks before the doctors and the pathologists and the neurologists and the oncologists decided that there was nothing they could do for him because they could not find what was wrong with him. He had left Kerch the money to come to Rome, dying just the month before. Casey was out of his room getting more tests when Kerch came to visit, but there was a man in his mid-to-late twenties in the other bed reading a biography of Natalie Wood.

"My name is Max. It is very lonely here, and I don't get many visitors. GMHC sent a buddy, but this was very hard for him. I was his first client. They should have started him out on someone healthier," he said. He held up a stuffed dog that must have been as old as its owner. "This is Curly."

He held the stuffed dog to his own face and looked it in a beaded eye. "I love Curly," he said, and then walked the dog over the hill of his knees.

It was an effort to look up and smile. Max was hardly more than a rag and a bone and a hank of hair. His skin was the color of fog. He could not eat because of abscesses in his mouth, he said, and had lost fifty pounds. His lover had died six weeks ago, both of his parents to cancer in the last year. A catheter implanted in his chest had exploded the first time it was used to give him a medication that might have halted at least one of his infections. Immediate open-heart surgery was needed to get the plastic pieces out of his body's most active muscle.

"So you see, Kerch," he said, "my life has been rather sad lately."

Casey, it seemed, was dying, and Kerch saw Max as a candidate to take his place. The greater the horror, the greater the suffering, the more remote the possibility that this would happen to him, Kerch often thought, as if these poor people were totems against the activity of the virus within him. But when Casey was brought back into the room, it was hard to tell which person would last longer.

"Are you a positive person, Kerch?" Max asked.

"I'm sero-positive. Is that what you mean?"

"No, I mean, are you positive about being positive?" Max asked with the earnest smile of a born-again Christian, as if the next question would be, Have you accepted Jesus into your heart as a personal savior?

"I have a good attitude about it," Kerch said. "Yes, I have a positive outlook."

"You have to structure it," Max said. "The mornings are best for meditation." He held up a little blue book that he kept on his nightstand. "These are meditations for people with AIDS. There is one written for every day of the year," he said. "And one of these days, I might just get over this hump."

Max laid his head back on his pillow as if on a layer of truth he had plumped up for himself. "Are you taking AZT yet, Kerch?"

"Not yet, though I'm thinking about it."

"You should, Kerch. You really should. It helped me a lot, but I can't take it anymore. My body just can't handle it," Max said. "You can see I'm something of a chatterbox. Well, at least I haven't lost my voice."

Kerch smiled for him.

"I don't hate my disease. I am loving it. That way, I help it to leave my body. There are only two emotions, Kerch, love and fear. I wish I could have told that to my parents. It's a good thing to know." And then he said, "I am at peace with myself, Kerch."

Kerch went up to him and kissed Max's forehead. "I can see that, Max. It was nice meeting you. Here's my number if there's anything that I can do for you."

"Ecco me," Kerch said.

Niccolo stood to embrace Kerch as he entered the Sora Lella. They kissed one another on the cheeks the way Italian men do, right there in public, which had a comforting effect. "I saw you cross the Ponte Fabricio. What took you so long to come into the restaurant?"

"I was sight-seeing," Kerch said.

A waiter came to their table and called them both Dottore, though Niccolo was the only one wearing a white lab coat. Kerch noticed that Niccolo, like so many Italian men of his class, was thin and elegant, although he had a slouch and was getting a stomach. "Will we practice your Italian or my English?" Niccolo asked.

"If I'm going to speak Italian, it will have to be in very, very simple sentence structures."

Niccolo smiled and said, "Good then, Dottore, my English. You are looking well. I always forget how handsome you are. How long has it been?"

"Seven years, eight. When you were in New York, just before the epidemic," Kerch said. "And your father, how is he? Have you persuaded him to give up his practice yet?"

"Not exactly. He'll take on clients who are as old as he is," Niccolo said. "He's in Ferrara trying to get a chair established to study and preserve a Jewish culture that seems to be disappearing in towns like Parma and Modena. What the Nazis didn't destroy, it seems that time has neutralized. We won't expire at the gates of our libraries like the Alexandrians did, but stumbling out the doors asphyxiated by the dust and library paste."

"I was shocked—when was it? two years ago?—when the synagogue was bombed."

"No, longer ago than that. I was sitting right here, as a matter of fact," Niccolo said. "I ran out to see what I could do, and a man came stumbling down the steps of the synagogue clutching the body of a child. He stood there and cried out, '*Siamo anche Italiani.* We have been here since Caesar.' Well, you might imagine the scene yourself. Have you eaten here before? Any of the house specialties are good. Why are you smiling like that? You look like you're going to cry."

The waiter had set down a basket of bread, and Kerch had cracked open a rosetta, a crusty bun that tears apart in mouth-proportioned pieces, each part as fleshy as the plump of one's hand. "I haven't had one of these in years."

Kerch described the graffiti on the Ponte Sisto. "The red

was painted by the Communists," Niccolo said, "the footnote
in black was done by the fascisti."

"Doesn't it disturb you?"

"It offends me, yes, but you know, the hate is so ancient,
so irrational, it seems to exist only in the past, like the atrocities
that happened in the Colosseum, or the sacking of Jerusalem
by Titus. Well, maybe not that ancient, but the Italians who
are anti-Semitic haven't even met a Jew, or wouldn't know one
when they did. Even Mussolini's heart wasn't in the depor-
tation, and he regretted what part he had in it."

"Oh, I suppose that would make him a humanist in the
Italian tradition."

"Suppose we change the subject," Niccolo said. "I'd much
rather talk about you. What else did you see today?"

Kerch's pleasure at seeing Niccolo tapered off. Being with
him had always been like sitting in a dark room with a mirror;
it takes and gives nothing back, but you know it's there because
you saw it before the lights went out. Even in bed with him,
Kerch thought he might as well be alone, might as well be
making love to himself, and so he'd lay claim to Niccolo's
body—this is what I would do to myself if I could—and licked
and smelled, and was wordlessly affectionate, because finally,
it was someone else's body, someone else's smell.

"I went to see the restoration of the Sistine Chapel," Kerch
said. "I got there early, just like when I was a student, and
tipped the guard so that he would let me lie on the floor to
look at the ceiling."

"How far along are they?"

"About halfway through the Creation."

"It must have been like seeing it for the first time," Niccolo
said. "You'll have to come back for the Last Judgment."

"All of the city seems more articulated to me. I must have
been half-asleep when I was here the first time, or I walked
around with one eye closed."

"You were often wrapped up in yourself. I often felt as if
we had to plan our days around your moods."

"Well, I don't seem to be capable of those depths of un-happiness anymore," Kerch said.

"You were young," Niccolo said. "The Italians would say that you needed a mule's swift kick to the back of the head."

"I rather liked your father's prescription better, though I could have used a stronger dose."

Niccolo missed a quarter beat, hardly enough for a singer to breathe before a note. "Are you here alone?" he asked.

"Yes, what of it?"

"Just that the city closes up at seven-thirty. People go home to their families. There really isn't anything to do here by way of meeting people when you are by yourself, you know, no bars, no clubs. I'd hate to see you get lonely."

"I don't suppose that is something you would see," Kerch said, and was silent. If the food hadn't been brought, if it hadn't been so delicious, he might even have wept. He felt as if he had been reprimanded, judged and found wanting.

"Did I tell you that I am getting married?" Niccolo asked.

"Married? You? Surely that isn't expected of you, not your parents."

"My mother passed away," he said. Kerch said he was sorry. Niccolo shrugged. "And my father is not going to live forever. Once he's gone, I'll have no family. I don't want to grow old alone."

"And your fiancée?"

"She's a wonderful girl," Niccolo said.

"Girl? She's only twelve?"

"We have much in common. She loves poetry," he said, "and she's ready to have children."

Kerch raised his wineglass in salute. "You will be a fine parent, I'm sure. Will you keep a boyfriend on the sly, or does one just assume that sort of thing?"

"I haven't thought that far ahead," Niccolo replied.

An older man at another table slapped the table, and his hand rose quickly in a precise and emphatic gesture up to his head. The three younger men at the table laughed, as did the waiter who was standing there. They looked like family. The movements of the old man's hands fascinated Kerch. The man picked up an orange with one hand and a sharp knife in the other. Even Niccolo turned to watch.

"He is saying that in his day we did not need amniocentesis to determine a child's sex," Niccolo translates. "The midwife would just take an orange and carve a little baby out of the rind over the woman's stomach." Kerch could see the old man carving the baby's head, his arms and legs, then he began to tear the limbs and body away from the pulp of the fruit.

"This is an old joke. I've seen it before," Kerch said. When the bambino was pulled away from the fruit of the orange, the core in the center stuck out like a long, thin penis. The other men at the table, and even the waiter, rolled their eyes and looked away.

"I do think about you," Niccolo said over the second course, "especially now."

Kerch didn't know what he meant. "Now that you're getting married, you mean."

"No, I mean the epidemic. I've wondered about your health."

"Oh, that." Kerch told him everything. "My doctor hasn't said it in so many words, but I think he'd be relieved if I started taking AZT."

"I think I would agree with him."

"Yes, but you're in the medical mode."

"As opposed to?"

"The spiritual mode," Kerch said. "There's a movement abroad, part of the new age, which says that fear causes illness, or lack of love, or fear of love. Even sick people have told me that worrying about AIDS would ensure my getting it, as if illness were punishment for impure thoughts. And I've been told by the healthy not to spend so much time helping the sick, because everyone is responsible for their own lives."

"You Americans, with all your freedom," Niccolo said, "are afraid to admit that you aren't in control of everything."

"I am not often afraid," Kerch said. "I've known for years that I was sero-positive, but I do have moments of paralysis, when I feel as if I have awakened to the sound of thieves ransacking my apartment, that they are about to come into my room and shine a flashlight in my face to see if I'm asleep. If nothing else, I would like to feel safe again, know how to think about the future."

"You live for the day," Niccolo said, "and plan for the long haul."

"I saw the Monte Testaccio yesterday for the first time," Kerch said, referring to an ancient mound of shards of amphorae, which were shattered to discharge their contents of oil, wine, and grain at the nearby river port.

"It's beautiful, isn't it?"

"I read where they used to drive oxen and swine off of it during festivals for swordsmen to kill."

"Really?"

"Then I visited the Protestant Cemetery," Kerch said.

"You always liked it there."

"Yes, I once wanted to be buried there under an obelisk."

Niccolo said, "That would have been an appropriate memorial, as I recall."

Kerch said, "I was wondering if they still sold plots."

"I suspect that you would have to have a significant connection to Rome to be buried there."

"Yes, that's what I was thinking, too," Kerch said. "Do you think that you could find out for me?"

"And if they don't, I mean, I'm sure that they haven't buried anyone there in years," Niccolo said. "And, if they did, the bureaucracy it would entail!"

"Maybe you could spread my ashes there. Could there be anything wrong with that, if they don't catch you?"

Niccolo said, "Why don't I just toss your urn against the Monte Testaccio with the rest of the broken amphorae."

Kerch said, "Because it would probably just bounce off."

"What if I just toss fistfuls of your ashes around your

favorite sites, how about that, in the Forum, on the Campidoglio, in Trastevere and the Borgo."

"I wouldn't want to be any trouble," Kerch said.

"You wouldn't even know you were in Rome."

"It's not a trip I look forward to."

"Really, Kerch, you still have this morbid streak. Even
Shelley said that that cemetery could make you half in love
with death. You're just excited about being back in Rome.
When you are back in New York, you will change your mind."

Kerch said, "That's why I bring it up now, Niccolo. If
you told me now that you would . . . You're right, it won't
matter then." He suspected that he had committed a social
faux pas by asking Niccolo to see to his remains; people are
more loyal to a dead man's requests if they are not facing him
over lunch. "I'm sorry I upset you. That was asking a lot."

The waiter set a glass of Sambuca down in front of
both of them. Niccolo raised his and said, "To your health,
then."

Kerch walked up the steps of the cordonata to the Campidoglio, as opposed to the parallel steps of the Aracoeli, where
he was actually heading. The steps to the church were too
many and too steep. There were 122 of them and they had
been built in 1348 as thanks for sparing Rome the brunt of
the Black Death, which had killed over half the population of
Florence and ravaged most of Western Europe. The number
of steps and their steep incline symbolized life as a dreary ascent
to heaven; pilgrims still climbed it on their knees, he'd been
told.

Marcus Aurelius was gone. That was the first thing Kerch
saw when he stepped onto the Campidoglio. Michelangelo
had designed the piazza as a pedestal for Aurelius and his horse.
Once the nostrils of the horse had poured wine and water
during a festival, and supposedly the horse's forelock would
sing to announce the end of the world, but from where, no
one now knew. The statue was said to be beyond repair. Acid

rain had rotted it, inside and out, and there were no funds to replicate it. But the Romans didn't seem to mind so very much. The piazza was still beautiful without it, and they felt the statue had been spared once already from the crucible that melted all pagan statues to cannonballs; Marcus Aurelius had been mistaken for Constantine, the first Christian emperor, instead of the pagan that he was; that is how the statue had survived. And maybe he got even more than he deserved. Originally, a bronze barbarian stood beneath the horse's hoof, and in more recent times, the fascists had declared the statue an enormous influence on modern art, though on whose art and what had been forgotten. Marcus Aurelius had had his extra centuries in the sun; his day was gone, but this made Kerch sad, as if it said that Rome was not eternal after all, or that eternity fed on the fodder of memory and memorials; the empty spot seemed even more a memento mori than the winged skeleton at the church on the Via Giulia.

A priest was coughing on the altar of the Aracoeli. He crossed it in a long black bathrobe, his chest bare to the damp cold. In a back chapel was the Santo Bambino, supposedly carved from the wood of an olive tree from the Garden of Gethsemane. There were a handful of letters stuck in front of its glass case, sent by the sick, mail-order prayers. Once, the infant had had its own carriage, which carried him to sickbeds and hospitals. Even fascist soldiers believed in its powers, and had let it pass through a crowd that had gathered to hear Mussolini speak. But to Kerch, the baby Jesus, swaddled in gold lamé and covered with cheap-looking jewelry, was a tacky little drag queen dressed for bingo in Cherry Grove. He covered his mouth when he started to laugh, and a nun entered the chapel with holy cards. She must have seen tears in his eyes, for she whispered, "Such devotion in one so young."

Kerch continued on down the Via del Corso, weaving in and out of the streets, window-shopping. He had not packed much; he had planned to buy. He was not going to deny himself anything to which he took a liking, as he'd done when he was young and had to tell the shopkeeps that a sweater was *"troppo caro per me, sono un pauvro studente."*

And yet he didn't see anything that he wanted, as if his ability to want things had atrophied, or that this season's fashions, the bright aqua, for example, or the blowsy denim shirts, could neither contribute nor augment the image he had finally come to of himself; and in that, he was somehow out of time, out of step.

That was how he felt back home, out of step with the fashionable vocabulary, where a person with AIDS was not sick but surviving, as if severe damage to the immune system was an auto accident from which they had walked away— done, over, complete in and of itself, the danger passed— instead of an ongoing condition with all its variables and vagaries. He and Casey were watching television one night when a person with AIDS said that he was not a victim, and Casey, who would be dead in a week, said, "I don't know about him, but I feel like a victim. I didn't choose this." It was as if the only way to rationalize the confusion of the world was to control the language used to describe it.

"Oh, but it's empowering," Kerch was told at a party where he had had too much to drink and become contentious.

"Empowering," he said. "If I was really empowered, I would make this all go away."

Then a woman in her mid-twenties pounded her chest with an open palm, squared out her chin at him, and with her eyes bulging screamed, "I feel empowered inside."

He had raised his hand and said in a staccato shout, "Duce, Duce, Duce." Empowering, he thought, if people were empowered by merely changing the way something was called, how weak were they really, how illusory was language?

And then there was the Quilt touring the country like a movable wake, panel upon panel of fabrics stitched together like a foldable, dry-cleanable cemetery. Seeing a beautiful man reduced to a name sewn on a bedspread had made him call a woman friend, an artist, to say, "Karen, you're the only one I'd trust with my panel." She said to him, "Why don't I make one up now and you can sleep with it."

At Casey's instigation, he went to a group called Body Positives to hear how others were dealing with being infected. "I've had a hundred and twenty-five friends die of AIDS," the team leader said. "They all led very stressful lives, so it's no wonder they got sick. I take a lighthearted attitude to the whole thing, but that's the reality I created for myself."

The team leader put on a tape made by a woman who had written a book that told people they could heal themselves. "I believe that we are one hundred percent responsible for our lives," the woman said. "Our health is a mirror of what we believe about ourselves. The very fact that you have found this tape and have discovered me means that you are ready to make a new positive change in your life. Acknowledge yourself for this." There was a silence of several seconds, and then, "The past has no power over us. The past has no power over us," she said with a lift in her voice. "Isn't it wonderful to realize that this is a new moment, a fresh beginning."

The team leader was smiling like a child with his head on his mother's lap, when she has returned home from a day in the factory. But another man stood and started to leave the room. "Excuse me," he said, "but this isn't what I came here for."

"If you don't intellectualize her," the team leader said, "she can be very helpful."

"I'm glad that it works for you," the fellow said as he headed toward the door. Kerch was going for his coat, as well.

The team leader said, "All she is saying is that you have to love yourself."

"No," the man said at the door, "I read her book. She says that AIDS is caused by self-hatred."

"Some gay men do hate themselves," the team leader said.

"You'd pretty much have to to believe this stuff."

The leader turned to the rest of the room and said, "She just doesn't want to see anyone get sick."

Kerch met up with the man on the steps. "Are you all right?"

He said, "I hate that metaphysical snake oil."

"It gives them a sense of control."

"Spiritual fascism."

"You can't take away their hope," Kerch said, arguing their viewpoint, though he didn't know why. "You can't deny the power of a positive outlook."

"Yeah, and an addict loves his drugs."

"They'd call you negative. They'd say you're a cynic."

"A cynic is a romantic gone sour," the man said. "I never did that."

"If you have all the answers already, why did you come tonight?" Kerch asked.

"I don't have all the answers. I wanted to know how others were handling this. I wanted to talk about issues, like do you tell someone you just met in a bar that you're sero-positive before you go home and have sex? Or do you wait on the chance that he wants to see you again, and then how do you tell him? I'm of a generation of gay men who never even needed to know another man's name to have sex with him."

Leaning against the opposite walls of the building's foyer, they stopped and faced each other. Kerch himself sometimes felt that the world was being divided into the HIV's and HIV-not's. Tell a man in a bar that you were sero-positive and he would look you in the eye, squeeze your arm, thank you for your honesty, wish you luck, and excuse himself to a distant corner.

"Well," Kerch said, "I don't know your name, but I do know you're sero-positive."

In the long pause, the man looked Kerch over with a slow-dawning, lopsided smile. "You live around here?"

"Yes, but I've got a sick roommate," Kerch said.

"Now I recognize you. You're the guy with the dying room," the man said.

"That's what the press called it."

The man put one arm out, leaned forward, and caught himself on the wall above Kerch's shoulder. He looked down into Kerch's face. "There's one other thing I'll ask you. Do you think oral sex is an acceptable risk?"

"It's one I'm willing to take," Kerch said. "If you let me."

Finally, in the church of Santa Maria del Popolo, Kerch found himself back in front of the Caravaggio, *The Conversion of St. Paul.* He opened his *Companion Guide* and read, "So much has been written about it, and it has been so frequently reproduced, that any comment seems superfluous."

He almost said, Don't fail me now. He had an impulse to shake the guidebook for more information, as if more history would come fluttering out of the bindings, like notes, or roses, or a dollar bill stuck between the pages. There was no one else in the chapel. Kerch put the *Companion Guide* back into his bag. He pulled out a small flashlight he had brought from America, because it was impossible ever to carry enough change in Italy for the light meters that illuminated everything one could want to look at.

There was Saul lying on the foreground where he had just fallen. He had been on his way to Damascus to find Jews who had been persuaded by the teachings of Jesus. He would root out these early Christians, the blasphemers, and they would be stoned until they collapsed and died. Kerch's teacher, Fink, had told them that the executioners would strip so as not to be encumbered by their clothes, and Saul stood guard over the clothes.

The moment in the painting varied wherever it appeared in the Bible. Saul is blinded by the light and hears the voice; his companions hear only the voice, or they see only the light. Here a servant's brow is lined with concern over the horse, not Saul. The perspective of the painting made the horse seem little more than a pony next to the servant, but compared to Saul lying on the ground, he is enormous. The saddle has fallen off the other side, the horse looks down at Saul, and Kerch laughed to paraphrase Frost's line: "My little horse must think it queer to stop without Damascus near."

Saul's arms were raised in a wide gresture, almost like one whose arms are being spread for a crucifixion. Yet his shoulders were beginning to relax, his knees were up and parted, his hips raised slightly, his mouth just open, like a man who is ready for his lover. He was an ugly man in Caravaggio's vision, ugly as a corpse; his eyes seemed rolled into his head like an epileptic having a seizure. His nipples were extraordinary and manly though, the body nice, his chest bare and his breeches pulled down as far as they could go without exposing him entirely. "If this is divine love, then I know it," someone had said of Bernini's *Ecstasy of St. Teresa,* her mystical union with Christ. The same could be said of this painting, Kerch thought. Not only know it, but to have been responsible for it as well, that moment of penetration when your lover looks at you, helpless with the knowledge that you have brought him to the edge of something, counting on you to maintain the moment, his security, his safety.

"For the sake of argument," Fink had said, "let's say that Jesus had come to Saul and told him everything he needed to know in that moment of light on the way to Damascus. Wouldn't Saul's own self-assigned role as executioner shape that revelation? Isn't it possible that love, all love, even the love of Jesus, can be misconstrued? Paul brought the arrogance and self-righteousness of an executioner to the new religion, tearing Christianity away from Judaism membrane by membrane," Fink had said, "certain he had a right to determine what the laws, the new codes would be. And Paul would be among the first to blame the Jews for killing Christ."

Kerch looked at the light on Saul's arms and across the horse's bulk. Surface into depth, the Italian trick, but the genius of the painting was not in the light, what use was a light that made the world fall back in shadow? Or was that the point?

Kerch considered the woman who wrote the book that said we were responsible for our own lives, that we could heal ourselves, that the past had no power over us. Hers was not the promise of life everlasting, but life now, if one would just believe her, if one would just believe in himself, if one would just love himself enough. Well, of course, he thought, who wouldn't take the guarantee of life now over the promise of life later? What in an unknown heaven could compare to what you had already developed a taste for—coffee in the morning, whiskey at night? So Kerch turned to leave the church, finished with Rome. There were cities he had never been to—Carthage, Alexandria, Babylon. The empty arms convinced him: Nothing remained but what remained to be seen.

for my doctor, N. Patrick Hennessey
"what lasts"
September 1989

THE
BODY AND
ITS DANGERS

=

I am aware of your body and its dangers.
I spread my cloak for you in leafy weather
Where other fugitives and other strangers
Will put their mouths together.

—THOMAS JAMES

My daughter is at an age: She is beginning to realize that she is the end result of something significant. Sex is not the issue; cause and effect is. She wants to know more about her father than I can tell her.

She resents how few men I have brought into her life. Marie and I had to take her out of public school because she was so obsessed with boys. A teacher caught her leading the other girls in song: "We are the girls of the fourth grade whore corps/We are the girls that the boys pay more for." My daughter thinks that lesbianism is next to laziness. She thinks this requires no effort.

My daughter also thinks that camouflage fatigues and army-surplus boots are fashions original to her generation, though I can't remember why I wore them, the uniform of the oppressor. Was it to protest the war, or was it the first stirring of a radical feminism? Though we may not remember our issues, there is no forgetting that we once had them.

My daughter will not wear contact lenses because she says they make her eyes too big. She complains that her neck is gangly. If she knew how beautiful she is, she would not worry about boys. She could sit in a window with a book or needle-point, and they would come to her. Of course, she hates it when I say such things.

What did I hate at her age? My name. And my sisters hated theirs: Rebecca, Ruth, Esther, Judith. Our mother loved our mournful names, redolent of Sunday school and the Old Testament. One pores over the book of Genesis to pick them out—they are rare. You have to assume the role of women, the wombs responsible for the sons of Japheth, the sons of Gomer, of Javan, Cush, and Nimrod. My mother named me Sara; I let her name my daughter Rachel, knowing that that would help her love a baby she saw as born in sin. I knew she would refuse to realize that abortion was an option I hadn't taken.

Rachel has accused Marie and me of making her father gay, which made Marie laugh until tears ran down her cheeks. But it hurts Marie, I can tell. She interprets Rachel's curiosity as incrimination. Rachel has kept us a family all these years—the way children are supposed to. If Marie had had a child of her own, perhaps she would not be dependent on me. Rachel calls Marie Mama, with the accent on the second syllable, and asks her questions about Papa, whom Marie also knew in the biblical sense. Timing and other accidents made Rachel my child, as opposed to hers. As it stands, it is almost as if Rachel was born to Marie, the way Sara bore Abraham their son Isaac. And if Gordon had been a woman, and I and Marie men, there wasn't a blood test invented at the time that could determine parentage.

Last year, for Rachel's fifteenth birthday, I visited the theater department where I met her father. In their archives, I found slides of a production we were in together, *The Garden*. There was a picture of him as Abel. (I'm hidden behind him —playing a sheep.) I had a picture made from the slide and presented it to Rachel. "Here's your father, darling," I said. Tears sprang to her eyes, and she cried out, "But he's just a little boy!" A conclusion with which I couldn't argue. Maybe the one I wanted her to make herself.

Children make you think less often of yourself, and illness makes you think of yourself all the time. Your body determines the subject of conversation, so to speak. I knew Rachel would never have a father; and Marie, saying Rachel would have something better—two mothers, à la Sean O'Casey—wanted her as much as I did. I think Marie prayed for a girl, a little Amazon.

I'm the Amazon now, one breast removed, no obstruction to the bow and arrow, if indeed there was anything I would shoot. That was six months ago. I am not long for the other breast, either, or it for me. Marie and Rachel have become like twin moons, their orbits closer to one another than to mine, though I know I hold them to me still. Marie has been going to women's music festivals and book fairs since my diagnosis, to lesbians in the arts and women in theater conferences, at Champaign-Urbana, in Madison, in Bloomington; she leaves on a Thursday, returns late on Sunday, taking Rachel with her, who usually abhors such things, the idea of them, the very thought of a separate world for women.

Of course, they both ask me whether I mind, if I will be all right. I say, go, go. I need to be alone now. There's healing to be done. So they leave thinking that they have satisfied my needs, and for three days Rachel will stop confusing the word *genesis* with *genocide* with *genetics*. If with her absence Marie betrays me, she does no more than my body has. I have yet to tell her that the cancer has spread to my bones, my lungs. What is left for it—the heart? Perhaps the body is just a shell, but what is there to make us think that except a body in a casket, death's process, or some disfigurement? In the mean-time, I am my body. And Marie loved me. I'm glad she did. I loved my body, too.

Irrevocable; a body part, once removed. And surface sen-sation where there is now scar tissue, as opposed to this drag I feel, the undertow and pressure beneath my own touch (who else's?), as if my fingers were really a hundred miles away. I was on the phone once, long distance, and I could hear two women in the background talking about their operations—the person to whom I was speaking could not hear them—and I was frightened because they were saying to one another that it is easy to let go. And I had a sudden sense that that which was lost, the irrevocable, the irredeemable, was right there on the phone line, as if the operator should have been able to get it back for me. And the operator should have been able to place Gordon, too, just beyond the voices on the other side of silence.

Our huge commodious apartment faces the lake. In this morning light, you think that all can be forgiven. But to forgive yourself your youth is not to protect yourself against the on-slaught of what can be remembered, or even the tiny corpses that memory's cat drags in. I had a friend who died last year. His name was J. Eli Altgeld. He was a psychotherapist who, in the last year of his life, discovered Zen Buddhism and decided that the past is all an illusion. I laughed when he told me so, and said, "It's a damn good thing you've given up your practice."

This question remains unresolved between us. For if the past is an illusion, and your future is foreshortened—even if I beat this thing, and I think I can—what do you make of the present, the condensed, the concentrated moment? Rachel is the only thing to come out of my life that was not a dissertation, a thesis, an argument, an analysis, a history, a biography, a rebuke. If the past is all illusion, what is left to her of me?

"Marie, maybe there's something I ought to tell you," Gordon said to her that November Thursday afternoon she seduced him. It was dusk; the deed was done. "I'm gay. I thought you should know."

The first snow of the season was falling and sticking. The branches of the campus maples were not entirely bare, and snow had dusted clusters of reddish brown leaves. The lake beyond the university was still blue, and still calm except for the occasional wave that broke itself upon the college walk. Ours was a city campus built in the anticipation that Lake Shore Drive would extend all the way to Wisconsin, instead of falling short of the new campus by twenty blocks. And so the chapel, Madonna della Strada, was streetless. The squat and solemn red brick buildings, which faced the lake, were always entered through a back door. The parking lot was the heart of the campus.

Marie lit a cigarette. She knew already. This would be the second such confession she had heard in a semester, the third in a calendar year. She had had to open her blouse for him, undo her own overalls. She had to take his hand and place it on her breast.

"Marie," he whispered. "Marie, did you come yet?"

"Yes," she said, "yes, three times."

"Oh," he said. "Can I come now?"

He was gay, she thought, but a stiff prick has no conscience. She took him in her hand and held him like the handle of a hammer or a wrench. She liked the weight of it. She could have him again, go on for hours. She had actually come four times, but she wouldn't tell him that.

"I have to go," he said. "I'm late for rehearsal."

"Come back," she said. Whatever urgency she had felt earlier had burned off, but she still wanted to lie back in bed and have him fuck her while she pretended that she was all alone. She wanted to be serviced.

"I won't be finished until after visiting hours," he said.

"You'll have to climb in through my window. You can stand on my shoulders."

"What about the Jesuits next door?"

"They'll have to wait until I'm finished with you. I just had my period and this is the last of my free days."

"I was wondering about that," he said. "You don't use anything?"

"Only the rhythm method as prescribed by the Pope and Mother Theresa."

But what did Gordon know of that, except what the priests had told him in the seminary where he had spent his adolescence? And what did they know of women's bodies, of ovulation, of menses?

"I'm not climbing through your window," Gordon told her.

"Okay, don't," she said. "Mother told me there would be men like you."

"Men like me?" He must have swaggered a bit around the room, for men love hearing that they are just like other men, and the thought would never have occurred to him on his own.

"I like you, Gordon," Marie said, "but you try my soul."

I remember that night because Gordon was late for rehearsal. It was the night we were going to begin work on the Begatting sequence of *The Garden*. While we rolled around on stage recreating man's fall from grace, the Women's Chorus would recite, "And Adam begat Seth, and Seth begat Enosh, who begat Kenan. And Kenan begat Mahalal, who begat Jared, and Jared begat Enoch, who became the father of Methuselah."

We were sitting in a circle on the floor talking about sex, and Gordon ran in just reeking of it. The women he passed looked up and into the distance, like an animal smelling one of her own on the breeze.

Renata, the director, angry that he was late, told him that we had been talking about our memories of pubescence, and asked him point-blank about his own.

"I didn't have one," he said.

We all laughed; I actually believed him. Renata smiled

firmly, and said, "No, really, Gordon. It's important that you contribute to these discussions. You always sit there as if you were judging us."

"Well," he said, and we all turned and looked at him. There was always something disarmingly sad about his expression, like one of those tiny zoo animals kept behind glass in black light. And he never talked about himself the way the rest of us did.

"When I was in eighth grade, there was this boy," Gordon said. "Well, he wasn't really a boy, he was bigger than all the rest of us. Maybe six feet tall. I saw him once in the boys' room in a stall without a door. He looked back at me kind of surprised, and said, 'Hey, Gordon, what are you looking at?' And he smiled, and I thought, Gosh, he has beautiful teeth.

"One day, Les started a fight with another kid in the class when the teacher was out of the room. And this guy said something like, Hey, Les, blow me. Les got out of his desk and walked very slowly up the aisle. And he said very quietly, 'You want me to blow you? I'll blow you.' First, Les just stood over this boy's desk. He said, 'Don't be afraid, pull it out.' Then Les got down on his knees. He even put his arm around the back of this boy's chair and said, 'Take it out, Doug, it's okay, I'll blow you,' which he just kept on saying over and over in the nicest voice possible until the teacher came back into the room."

It was as if we had been talking about what we knew of death and Gordon had wheeled in a corpse. Marcus, who played Cain to Gordon's Abel, was staring at Gordon. It seemed to me even then that Gordon had said all this for Marcus's sake; the seeds of something were planted in his mind.

Memory's cat. When I remember Marcus, it is his naked back—the sight of him leaving my bed, the hair on his buttocks curved to the shape of his ass, and the sight when he knelt to pick up his trousers, the hang of his balls between his legs, and finally the sight of him leaving, aware of my presence behind him at the door. It was as if he was always *about* to turn around and say he loved me, or thought perhaps I might if he did, and was afraid of that. I would only have said that I loved the sight of him. But he didn't and I didn't, and I suppose that is why he returned to me and I to him, for what our bodies offered up. What I miss from those years are his comings and goings.

"I want to try something," he said, staring straight at Gordon. "I just want to try something in the Cain and Abel sequence." I saw Gordon smile a little and swallow, but it was apparent that he didn't know what to expect. Marcus put his arm around Gordon's shoulder and whispered an instruction. Gordon nodded.

A Woman of the Chorus stepped up behind them. They stepped onto the mats that helped to break Gordon's falls to the floor.

"Cain killed Abel, but Cain did not know that by killing Abel he would cause his brother's death," the Chorus Woman said. "And God said to Cain, Sin is crouching at your door; its desire is for you, but you must master it." Marcus began the murder scene, only more slowly that night. He crushed Abel's hands, arms, chest, abdomen and legs, but this night, with each punch, with each broken limb, Gordon kept his sad, dark eyes locked on Marcus's face, as if in submission, while the rest of us sat in a semicircle around them providing the sound effects for the crack of Abel's skull, the *whoosh* of air knocked out of his lungs, the breaking of his limbs with sticks and rhythm blocks, ratchets and cowbells, the musical instruments of kindergarten children.

Usually, Marcus just lifted Gordon up to God when Abel was dead, as if in sacrifice, but this night, Cain tried to put the life back into Abel's body. He brushed his hair; he opened Abel's mouth and blew into it to make his lungs rise. Marcus caressed Gordon's limbs, and put grass in them and tried to make the sheep eat from Abel's hands. Then Cain pulled Abel onto his lap and rocked him and whispered in his ear. Tears were dropping off Cain's face onto Abel's, and Marcus actually licked them off. The rest of us watched, riveted. Finally, Marcus stood up. He picked up Gordon by the front of his sweatshirt and lifted him so slowly that Gordon's limp body hung slack against his own. Abel's head fell back. Marcus opened his mouth as if to scream, the lips pulling back over his teeth. Instead, he pulled Gordon's face up to his own and kissed him harder than you can a living person. We could see his tongue slip into Gordon's mouth, could see the muscles of his neck. And Gordon, who was playing dead, could not respond. I saw one of his fingers lift and fall, as if striking a piano key, then Marcus dropped him to the floor, in a heap, and I suspect, in a swoon.

Rachel asks me what it was like when I was her age, meaning, of course, what it was like for me. And didn't I like boys? My sisters and I had jobs. I worked in a shoe store—it was good money—and I did children's theater in the summer. My father caught polio from one of us, after our inoculation. Who knew that we were contagious? My mother furnished the house with the insurance money. But comfort is not safety. She went into the hospital for a hysterectomy, and when she got out, recuperated on the new couch. She did not talk about it, and did not want us to talk about it. I did not know what the operation was until I was in high school many years later—I did not connect it to cancer. When I remember that time, we girls are standing in a line, looking down at her, waiting for her recovery.

In the last months of J. Eli Altgeld's life, I learned to keep a poker face for him, for he hated the anguished looks, the helpless pity, the unspoken question: Tell me what I can do for you? And I learned not to respond to his question: How are you supposed to live at the end? You agonize over every decision, he said, what should I remember, what should I forget?

He was a surrogate father to Rachel. She adored him and was furious with him for getting ill, and he was more comfortable with her anger than my concern. It was something that they shared. His death to AIDS was further proof to Rachel that we were doing something wrong by going against nature.

I'd say, "Biology is not destiny," and she would snap back, "No, chemistry is."

I think, The chemistry of attraction, odor, quickening pulses; the body and its dangers. I think of the chemistry of a virus that attaches itself to a cell and inserts its RNA to combine with that cell's DNA, killing its host and recreating itself many times over. I think of the chemistry of cancer cells that multiply in the tissues of my breast, overbreeding and traveling up to the pit of my arm as if following a map, illegal aliens looking for work. I think of the chemistry of my drugs, the chemical process that goes on after death. I think of chemistry that craves solitude, chemistry's recall, the chemical process of thought and will.

J. Eli Altgeld knew Gordon, also. We figured this out after I had started therapy with him, a few years after Rachel was born. Marie and I were asked to leave the women's co-op when they learned that I was seeing a man, a male psychotherapist. He will not know you, they told me, he will not be sensitive. He cannot be sympathetic. But I did not want someone to know me. I wanted distance, disinterest. I wanted to be new to someone, not history. Jake and I stopped analysis and went on as friends. There was never not knowing one another; there was never distance, never disinterest. I told him my story, he told me his, late into the night, volumes of wine and masses of deep-dish pizza our midnight oil.

"How did you know it was him?" I asked Jake. "With all the men you've had?"

"Something you said about the way he made love, the way he evaded questions," Jake said. "That one wasn't taking any prisoners."

And as Jake told me about Gordon, I could see him entering this room through the foyer where Jake used to have a photograph of a young boy taking a deep toke off a roach clip, of Gordon's feet not touching the floor when he sat on the chesterfield sofa, and even of Gordon in the bedroom upstairs.

They had met on the Friday after Thanksgiving. *The Garden* had rehearsed all day that day, and I wonder whether Gordon wasn't tired of us all by that time, our incessant confessions at the beginning of each rehearsal, our heterosexuality. Jake had found him as he was being turned away at the door of the neighborhood gay bar; he was not old enough to be served in Illinois at that time. And Gordon just loved to drink; he loved cognac, brandies, especially the rough stuff, like slivovitz and schnapps. Instead of going into the bar, Jake had followed Gordon down the street and offered him a drink at home.

"And he just accepted, just like that?" I asked.

"No, not until he saw where I lived."

"Do you live here all by yourself?" Gordon asked Jake on the steps of the town house that Jake owned.

"Most of the time."

"I've never lived alone."

Jake smiled at that and blinked down at him, the way I saw him do to Rachel when she expressed longing for something that he could provide her. "I confess, I've grown tired of it," Jake said, already fond of Gordon, that belying innocence.

Gordon's eyes would have been level with the porcelain bell pull outside the door. Jake would have rubbed the engraved plate beneath it with his elbow: DR. J. ELI ALTGELD. "Good Chicago stock," he'd say, as I had heard him say many times over.

Jake remembered the first thing that Gordon said when he drank from the wineglass he was offered. "You don't let this wine breathe; you give it artificial respiration."

I imagine Jake kneeling in front of the ancient prie-dieu

that had been transformed into a liquor cabinet and pulling out a bottle of cognac probably twice Gordon's age.

"Would you like to smoke a joint?" Jake would have asked, for we smoked so much back then.

"I don't know," Gordon said. "Grass makes me sleepy."

"All the sooner to go to bed," Jake replied, and opened the old sideboard where his stereo was kept and turned on a reel-to-reel tape player. The room was filled with a chorus of tenor voices singing Gregorian chant. Gordon would have listened for a moment and recognized the Mass being sung. He had never listened to chant as background music, and thought of it as sort of an aesthetic sacrilege.

"Are you Catholic?" Gordon asked.

"My family was." Jake asked, "When did you leave the seminary?"

"A few months ago. How did you know?"

"A lot of ex-seminarians around," Jake said, sitting down next to Gordon. "How does someone from the seminary have such cultivated tastes in alcohol?"

"The priests were generous if they liked you."

"And the priests liked you very much. Why did you leave?"

"It was a place to grow up."

"Where were you from before the seminary?"

"A Catholic foster home. Any more questions?" he asked. "I don't really like answering them."

"Why not?"

"There you go again."

"What should we do, then?"

Gordon paused a moment and said, "May I kiss you?"

Jake leaned over to oblige him. He had a lovely mouth. I've imagined he was lovely to kiss. Gordon would have felt the strong lips, a two-day beard.

"Why did you think you had to ask?" Jake said.

"I don't know," Gordon said. "Why did you pick me up?"

"I may offend you."

"I can hardly wait," Gordon said, his guard up.

"I'm attracted to boys."

Gordon was offended. "I am hardly a child," he said.

"I wouldn't have brought you home if you were," Jake said. "Would you like to smoke some more?"

"No," Gordon said.

"Some more brandy? Would you like to take it to bed?"

Jake took Gordon upstairs, then down to the bed, and pinned his arms at the elbows to the mattress. "Just be still," he whispered, undressing Gordon. He rolled his tongue slowly and firmly around Gordon's neck, down his spine, and worked his fingers into the wet skin left in the trail of his mouth. When Jake covered Gordon's mouth with his own, Gordon could taste himself on Jake's tongue, perspiration and cognac, like a salted, over-ripe apple.

"You're so easy to make love to," Jake said.

"I haven't done anything," Gordon said.

Jake used a lubricant that smelled of eucalyptus and cloves. He opened himself with his fingers, and straddled Gordon, sitting back and guiding him in at once. He smiled. "If the priests knew what they were losing when they lost you."

"You're making me come," Gordon said.

"Then I'll make you come again," he said, and covered Gordon's face with his large hand. And Gordon came and stayed erect. "I've never done this before," he said.

"Never fucked a man? Does that mean that no one has ever fucked you?"

Gordon laughed. "I guess it does."

"Do you want to try?" Jake rose off of him and positioned Gordon so gently and quickly that there was no way or time to refuse him. Gordon started to pull away when he felt Jake's beard against the crack of his buttocks, but Jake held him down until Gordon began to give way.

"The first time, it usually hurts," Jake said. "There's no hurry. Just try to relax."

Gordon said, "If I get any more relaxed, I'll be comatose."

Jake wrapped his arms around Gordon and lifted him onto his lap. Gordon leaned back into his arms. "You bring me in, little one," Jake said. "You help me find it."

Gordon had no idea of what he was supposed to find. "Now take a deep breath. Now take another. At your own speed now," he was instructed. Gordon dropped his head back to Jake's shoulder. He sat as deeply as he could and felt a cold weightlessness rise from his bowels and balloon into his head. He froze for a brief moment, and Jake smoothed the gooseflesh that had risen on his arms. Gordon felt as if he were opening up into nothing at all, that there was no difference between the cock inside him and his own in Jake's fist; but it scared him that what distinguished his inside from his outside had dissolved. He was hovering over that spot; a part of his body, not an inch thick, had exploded into consciousness a mile wide. He wanted the feeling to stop, and he didn't, the way you watch something valuable fall and break even though you might have moved fast enough to catch it, the way you stay with physical pain, experience it like a car ride, because there is nothing that can be done about it. He pushed his head into the crotch of Jake's throat; he sat down even deeper into Jake's lap, forcing the sensation, the distance between the physical and the not. And he began to rock. The Gregorian chant was coming into the bedroom through hidden speakers. "In thee I place my trust," the chorus sang. "I shall not perish. My foes shall not mock me."

Jake fell asleep after he came; his cock grew soft and slipped out of Gordon's body. Gordon would have gotten out of bed and walked through a dressing room into the bath, to wash and to explore the house. He lowered the light on the dimmer switch as low as it could go and he could still see. From a hook behind the door, he took a hooded bathrobe, which made him look like a monk. He sang into the mirror, *"Et cum Lazaro quondam paupere aeternam habeas requiem."*

"Are you all right?"

"Oh, shit." Gordon jumped. "I thought you were sleeping."

"I was," Jake said. "You were crying?"

"No, I was singing."

Jake looked at Gordon and did not speak. Eventually, he asked, "What are you doing in here?"

"You fell asleep."

"What if we got something out of the refrigerator and ate it in bed?"

"I think I should go back to my dorm," Gordon said.

"I don't want you to go."

Gordon had never seen a man who seemed so unaware of his nakedness. In the seminary, even in the dormitory, boys either covered themselves or paraded. There was one, he remembered, who used to stand on his bed while towel-drying his hair, his balls hanging low, his cock hanging over them, aware that everyone was looking at him as he himself looked out the window. The boy's body hair had been platinum, and he had a Roman nose. Gordon watched Altgeld's fingers as they moved from his breastbone to his groin.

"Are your parents still alive?" Altgeld asked.

"I don't know."

"Yes, you do."

"I think so," Gordon said.

"Can you remember them?"

"I remember my mother. There were lots of men. One of them may have been my father," Gordon said, feeling himself growing cranky. He was afraid if he began to cry, he would wake up in the morning with a cold. "Why are you asking all these questions?"

"I care to know," Jake told him. "Did you ever love anyone?"

"Isn't that a stupid question?"

"Depends on how you answer it."

Gordon thought, and said, "Yeah, my mother. But it didn't last."

Jake rubbed his hand across his furry chest; Gordon saw the weight of his balls shift in their sack. Jake said, "You don't know how handsome you are, do you?" Gordon pulled the hood of the bathrobe over his face. "And you're more willing in bed than you are in conversation."

"There aren't so many dangers in the body."

"How would you know?"

"Don't make fun of me."

"I wouldn't do that, Gordon."

"I'm too old to be your son."

Jake just said, "Come back to bed with me."

"I'm afraid I'll keep you awake."

"Then stay with me till I fall asleep. It won't take long, I promise."

Marie has not changed much in all this time. She hated leaving the co-op, I suspect, because as a child she envisioned herself growing up to be a nun, and the co-op was a reasonable realization of that dream. She did not blink an eye when they suggested she cut her long blond hair and dye it brown, because that would make her "look more like a dyke." When AIDS began killing her friends in the theater, she refused to become involved, swearing that gay men would not do as much for lesbians if the situation were reversed. "What about our health collective, what about our clinics?" she asked. It gains nothing to point out that we did not maintain them, that they had closed even before the epidemic began. She says that men would not give us money to keep them open, and I say that we didn't ask them, though I know that this is just a fraction of a long, difficult equation that contains variables like history and resentment, privacy and pride, progress and destruction. I think of my mother alone on the sofa, like a cat going off to die alone in the woods, telling us not to worry, which meant not to talk about whatever ailed that part of her we were never ever to talk about. The word *cancer:* some part of my Catholic-saturated, little girl's mind equated her illness with punishment—another thing we did not talk about after the fact—for having had too many children.

And I suspect that Marie does not become involved in AIDS or women's health because sex and death are just as hard for her to talk about as for anyone else. She maintains that it was Gordon who made her a lesbian, that she had never given a thought to such practices before he told her he was gay; she denies that feelings long repressed had anything to do with her decision to love women, to love me. It was an intellectual decision, she said, and Gordon was the catalyst.

"Marie," he said to her, "you cannot hold me responsible for such an effect on your life. That is not in anyone's power, let alone mine. Why do you try to make everything so simple when everything is not?"

"You think this was easy for me?" Marie asked.

"Not if you gave it any thought," Gordon replied.

She had dragged him back to tell him this, to tell him she was grateful. She had even dressed in her only skirt and blouse in order to come out of the closet. But most of all, she wanted to talk about me. How she had waited for me to get out of rehearsal, how we had gone out for a beer, and how she had struggled to tell me what she had just told him. I had wept, and left the bar when I realized that she was trying to ask me to come to bed with her, and that I had turned around and gone back to her for the very same reason.

It seems to me that memory is just a race to keep up with the past, and that what happened seventeen years ago has that much of a lead on me. Of course, I remember that night with Marie. I remember her on her knees, pushing my legs apart with her head, her hair across my thighs hiding her face from what she was doing—though I knew, God, I knew. My body rode on waves, tossed back and forth between the danger of what she was doing to me and the safety of it. St. Augustine said that what we know of the world, we know through our senses, but more than the world, it's how we know ourselves. Years ago, I asked J. Eli Altgeld why giving up sex in the face of a new disease would be so difficult, and he said, "Imagine never being penetrated again." "Unthreatened sexuality," he'd say, "what we learned from it." And I'd say, "It was never that for us, for women."

I did not know how to answer him, though, when he asked, "Not even for you and Marie?"

Rachel wants to know how it happened that she was conceived, and I say, "Oh, one thing led to another." What happened in between, I lie to her, falls away, forgotten. . . .

"I thought a long time about telling you this," Marie told Gordon. "Sara does not want to give up sex with men. She says she'd like to sleep with you. She says she loves your scene together in *The Garden* where you're supposed to be making love to her."

"Marie, that's not real."

"Be that as it may, if she's going to bed with anyone, I won't mind so much if it's you. That's what I really brought you here to say."

And then one day, Marie told him that I was having my period and that I didn't want to see her. "And she doesn't want to see me during her free days, either," Marie said. "She might call Friday, but I'm not waiting. Do you want to go to a midnight movie after your show Friday night?"

Gordon said, perhaps too slowly, "No, I don't think so, Marie."

Marie squinted at him, like a cat sniffing the breeze. "Just you be careful with her. She's small and you are not." Then she stood and left the table.

There was a scene in *The Garden* in which the entire cast snaked into the audience with apples, seducing them as Eve had been tempted. That Friday night, I was standing near Gordon when he bit from his apple and handed it to an older man, who said, "Thank you, my friend. You are beautiful."

It is true that there are people who are transformed by the stage—they do become beautiful, but they don't know it, for they see themselves in a mirror as others see them on the street. Their ordinary features become interesting—eyes darken, voices deepen, they seem taller. And when they walk across the stage, they absorb the empty space between you, and it seems as if you could reach out and touch them. Renata said that Gordon took the stage from all of us without knowing it. There was something devotional about him, priestly and sacred. It was Jake, of course, who had told Gordon that he was beautiful. No one had ever said such a thing to him; he returned to the stage before our cue and hid behind the proscenium arch until the rest of us returned.

During the Cain and Abel sequence, the audience gasped as each of his limbs, one after another, was shattered. He stared at Marcus, or I should say, Cain, as if he understood, as if he himself had something for which to apologize. Everyone onstage saw what he was doing, too, but I was the only one with the vantage point to see that Gordon stared blankly into the audience after Abel's last breath, which is why I suspect that his death met with open sobs. He didn't move, though, for the longest time, even after all the rest of the cast was in place for the next sequence, looking at him, waiting for him. Before we could go on, Marcus had to go over to him. He brushed his hand through Gordon's hair with tender deference and whispered, "Come on, buddy. Next scene."

As we started the copulation scene, I said to him, "Kid, you kill me sometimes."

He asked, "Can I walk you home tonight?"

"I'd like that," I said. I figured that Marie had set us up.

He walked me home and I rewarded him with a glass of whiskey from the bottle another lover had left there, and I left him alone while I changed. I lit a candle so that when Gordon walked into my room, the flame projected my body against my nightgown. There was a light coming in from the street, which I stepped onto like a stage. When Gordon entered, I

pulled a string on my nightgown and it slid down my body
to the floor. Gordon did not laugh, though I had meant him
to. I think in the tinny light from the street, my body must
have glowed as white as fish that evolve in caves. We mirrored
one another in a game that young actors are taught: What I
did to him, he did to me, repeating my action with a slight
variation.

He started to enter me, standing there in the middle of
the room. He looked at me, a little surprised. "Marie is so
easy," he started to say.

"She is bigger than I am, yes." I smiled.

"And wet," he said.

I backed up until I felt the bed against the back of my
legs and I sat down. I pulled on Gordon's arm to make him
kneel in front of me. I put my hand on the back of his neck
and made him part my legs with the top of his head. He
hesitated with a quick glance to my face. I felt his evening
beard against my thighs, and I thought to tell him that a full
beard would add years to his face. In the meantime, he was
just a boy making me feel as soft and wet as the meat of a
plum.

I stretched back to the bed and took Gordon's head between my hands and made it move and stop where I wanted
it to, the places that I thought he wouldn't take the time to
find. I said, "I want you to run your mouth over my body,
and I will tell you where you missed." I did not have to guide
him for long, but I held his head while he did what he was
told. All he missed was the top of my breasts. I brought him
inside me when I was ready for it, and when he asked me if I
had come yet, I said no, and no, and no. And he stayed erect
after he had come twice himself, young that he was, little that
he knew. All he asked from me was that I straddle him. I think
now of what Jake had said to me about never being penetrated
again, never being broken open; I knew what he was saying
then, and did not want to give it up.

"Do you know the story of Sarah and Abraham?" Gordon

asked me when we were done. He made the sound of my name erotic, made me want to start all over again. "God came to Abraham when he was ninety-nine years old and told him that Sarah would bear him a child. And Abraham fell on his face —it even says so in the Bible—and laughed. 'Shall a child be born to a man who is a hundred years old? Shall Sarah, who is ninety years old, bear a child?' "

"Where was she during all this?"

"Oh, she was listening in the tent. She laughed, and said, 'After all these years, shall I again have pleasure?' "

I rubbed my hand under the hardness beneath Gordon's balls, then smelled my fingers. "I love the way a man smells here," I said.

He smelled himself on my fingers and said, "So do I." Then he laid his hand on me and said, "I once heard a priest refer to this as the Mound of Venus. I half-expected to see her rise from the dugout and wind up for the pitch."

"You know what Marcus calls the women's dorm?"

"No," he said.

"The Venus de Milo Arms." The way he laughed made me think it was safe to ask him, "Gordon, that story you told us about Lester . . . did that really happen?"

"No," he said.

"You were trying to seduce Marcus, weren't you?" He smiled. "Did you succeed?"

"I can hardly kiss and tell now, can I?" he said.

"You don't answer any questions you don't choose to, do you?"

"Was that a question?" he asked.

Gordon was gone before I woke the next morning. In the kitchen sink, I found a saucepan in which he had heated himself some milk and corrupted it with some brandy that I happened to have.

The sun is so low in the sky that it holds steady across our windows for the better part of the day. An afghan is ready for the moment the sun moves west, leaving me in the cold shadow our building will cast. It will be dark in this room while the lake surface still glows in the near distance.

It does nothing to think of the past as a foreign country, nor as our near distance, nor as Jake said, an illusion; it is false comfort to believe that memory is willed and selective, like the muscles of your body you can control—fingers, tongue—as opposed to the ones you can't—your heart. Waves continue to rise and fall even in a frozen lake. They pulse up against the plate of ice, keening and rasping, asthmatic and captive. Ice breaks against the foundations of our building. You can hear it if you put your ear against the wall; you can hear it in your pillow.

Abortion was legalized just months after Rachel was born. I worked in an abortion clinic for a while that year. We kept a book of nightmares, of abortions we had witnessed in our dreams. In our dreams, everyone had them—our fathers, boyfriends, professors. Aborted fetuses chatted and gossiped like hairdressers; they knew us and told our secrets, our lies, and predicted our futures like tiny oracles. Sometimes we just laughed at the sheer horror of the dreams, for they were never really half as odd as our waking reality. Catholic women demanded that we baptize their fetuses; pagans, Jews, it didn't matter who did it, as long as someone said, "In the name of the Father, the Son, the Holy Spirit." I imagined the souls we blessed flying straight to heaven, like putti to the feet of the Virgin.

We had a labor strike at the abortion clinic. There were doctors who inevitably caused a woman pain during an abortion, and there were doctors who never did. We wanted the former to watch the latter, and they refused, as if pain were price. When someone on the picket line said that a graduate program was starting at the University of Chicago, an interdepartmental discipline called Women's Studies, I left the line to telephone for information. I figured I had as much to offer as to learn: lesbian mother, abortion counselor, witness to this violence.

But I get ahead of myself.

I didn't tell Marie when I missed my period, maybe because I was half-expecting her to ask. She had hoped that with all the motion of our bodies, one against the other, that our cycles would begin to come together. The only one I told was Renata. "I need a doctor," I told her. I assumed that she would know of an abortionist.

When she looked me in the eye, I knew that she knew that Gordon was the father; I even saw her take responsibility, as she had brought us together in *The Garden*. "I'll have to make some calls," she said. "Don't worry."

The doctor she found for me was in Skokie, a long, lonely ride on the El. I called and made an appointment for the test, assuming another appointment would be necessary for the abortion. I kept thinking of the difference in our ages, Gordon's and mine. He was eighteen; I was twenty-one and felt so much older than he. The doctor's practice was in his own home. I entered through the front door, passed through the dining room and its breakfront full of silver and china, down to what would have been, in any other house, the family room.

There were other women waiting, all older than I was, the youngest by ten years, the oldest by twenty. None of us had brought a friend along, and none of us spoke to one another. What we were doing was illicit. When each woman was finished in the doctor's office, she was led by a receptionist and nurse to a curtained cubicle, where she could lie down for an hour before going home. Each of them clutched her purse to her stomach as she was brought out. I hadn't yet begun to wonder how much this was going to cost.

By the time it was my turn, the other women were gone, which I regretted, thinking that I might need one of them. I had seen a gynecologist only once in my life. I did not know what to expect as I lay on the examination table. I looked about the room as the doctor examined me. There was my urine specimen on the table. There were his diplomas. His full name was Seymour Kline. I watched the hands on his clock move just for something to do. Five minutes passed. I said to myself, Well, they don't call him Seymour for nothing. Dr. Kline said it would take a few more minutes. Suddenly, I was scared. What did he see? Was there something wrong with me, cancer like my mother, was it possible that I couldn't have children, after all? There was something in his touch and something in his long controlled breaths that made me sit up onto my elbows.

"Scared?" he asked.

I wanted to say, A little, but he took one of my hands and placed it on his groin. "Maybe this is what you need," he said.

I pulled my hand back and sidled off the table and dropped to the floor. My clothes were in the corner on the chair. I put them on with my back to him.

"You'll have to call me in a few days for the test results," he said, "though I could do a D&C right this moment, if you want. Save you the time and trouble of coming back."

Fully dressed, I turned as if I had heard concern in his voice. "You'll call, won't you?" He really wanted to know. "I have to know if I'm going to test this specimen."

"Oh, Master Gordon," Marie exclaimed in the voice of an old nun she called Sister Jerome. I was in my room; she was answering the door. "You got my note, little one. Let me take your jacket. Oh, I am afraid that this is not warm enough for our devilish winters. Are you hungry? Sister Maximilian is calling out for a deep-dish pizza. I think she has her eye on the Protestant delivery boy, poor lost soul. And there may even be a beer in the Westinghouse, if Sister Sebastian did not drink it with her cheese fondue."

"How long have you been staying here, Marie?"

"A week. I haven't moved everything in yet. Sara's in the bedroom. Go in and see her. I'll be back in an hour."

I was sitting back in the corner at the head of the bed. I had called Kline back that afternoon for my test results. He told me, "If you need anything else, call. A lot of women do, you know."

Gordon shook one of my feet and smiled. I was wearing

flannel pajamas. "Marie gave them to me for Christmas. They even have a flap in the back," I said. "I gave her a Swiss army knife. It's what she wanted."

He sat on the edge of the bed to show me what he had just bought. "I was in the bookstore and this girl came up to me and said that she had seen *The Garden* three times. It moved her to reread all her favorite children's books. She suggested that I buy these two. She said they're classics." I could see that Gordon had spent maybe thirty dollars on the books. "But this one I picked out myself," he said. *"Dick Whittington, Lord Mayor of London."*

I was watching his face as he told me the story of an orphan who sold his cat to a king for an enormous fortune, and who heard the church bells ring his name before he ran away: Dick Whittington, Dick Whittington, Lord Mayor of London.

"It even says the stone he sat on when he heard the bells ring is still there," Gordon said. "I really shouldn't have bought this. I don't have a penny to my name, and I've been accepted into the Rome Center for next year."

"How will you afford it?"

"My scholarships will transfer. I really only have to make enough money for traveling expenses. I'm going to get a job in a grocery store. My roommate makes a lot of money that way. You should see his stereo."

I swirled red wine around in my glass. I could feel it making my face burn. "I wish I didn't have to tell you this, Gordon. I'm pregnant and the baby is yours, although I wish it wasn't, if only for your sake."

Gordon's lips parted slightly. He looked down at the books in his lap and must have seen the irony of their purchase. He held them up and attempted a self-conscious, self-mocking laugh. Instead, a short moan rose high in his throat. I took the books and placed them on the bed.

"I'm sorry," he said.

"I'm sorry I did this to you."

"I thought you couldn't that night."

"I should never go by that."

"What do you want me to do?"

"Marie wants me to have the baby," I said. "We want to have the baby. It's going to keep me from going to graduate school for a year, but I can wait. I told Marie that I can't have your baby without your permission, though."

"Then you've considered an abortion."

"Yes, Marie said we could split the cost three ways. She feels responsible."

Gordon was silent, then said, "Marie told me that you and Marcus did it the night before we did."

"Marcus never came inside me."

We sat in silence. I waited for him to say something just so that we would be able to talk. I wanted to tell him about Dr. Kline and the other women in his waiting room, the skimpy curtains that hid them and whatever they were feeling from the others. Marie and I had spent the entire day laughing one minute and crying the next over our predicament; I wanted to pull him into my life the way a novel draws you into its story, the way your eyes are drawn into the empty branches of winter trees. Finally, I said, "Gordon, you're making me feel so alone."

He said, "I just realized that my mother must have been pregnant when I saw her last."

I filled my glass with wine and gave it to him. Marie had left her cigarettes; I lit two and gave one to him. I knew nothing of this. He never spoke of his mother during *The Garden* rehearsals the way the rest of us had. "When was that?" I asked.

"I don't know. How old are you at the end of the second grade?"

"Seven or eight."

Then it had been ten or eleven years since he had seen his mother. I assumed that she had died, killed in a car accident, or struck by a hunter's stray bullet when she stepped out into her backyard to ask him not to hunt near her house. For a moment, I thought of the injustices in the world, if cars were safer, if guns outlawed. I didn't know what to say except, "How old was she? Was she pretty?"

"About your age. No, probably twenty-three. And she may have been beautiful. We were staying with a friend of hers, an older woman who had a small house and a large yard. Winter was over. I remember the new grass had grown through the old. There was a huge apple tree filled with blossoms. My father, whoever he was, had left us, and we had no place to go. My mother hadn't taken me to school in several days, and I was afraid that I would have to repeat the second grade. But what I remember most about the day, other than the color of the grass, was her dress, which was white, and which brought out her freckles. She wore very little makeup, or at least I don't think she did. She was sitting at a picnic table in the backyard and I climbed up on the bench across from her to see what she was doing. She was filling out an application to St. Michael's Guardian Angel Home, an orphanage. Across the top of the application, it said, 'Suffer the Little Children to Come unto Me.' Beneath that, she had printed my name.

"There were three more applications for my brother and sisters. My mother looked up at me and smiled. I knew from her smile that she wanted me to smile back, for if I cried, she'd change her mind. And she didn't want me to change her mind, so it was easier for me to say nothing and to turn away."

"What about your brother and sisters?" I asked.

"Oh, them," he said.

"Don't you keep in touch?"

"The nuns separated us from one another. Sometimes I'm afraid that they'll find me. You read about that kind of thing all the time."

I said, "I think I should have the abortion, Gordon. Marie and I have enough money for it."

As soon as I said it, I knew that I was going to keep the baby. I knew that I was lying to him. I decided not even to tell Marie until it was too late to do anything about it. I would tell her when I could no longer hide it; I would tell her that the baby would be ours, there would never be any reason to tell Gordon. What did we need a man for? Our baby would never want for a father. Marie had already promised to stick with me, through sickness and in health. And if we timed it right, Gordon would never know.

For I knew if I told Gordon that I wanted the baby, he would stay in Chicago, and I knew if I told him that I would have an abortion, he would be freed to go to Rome, rid of one another, or at least, me of him. "I'll pay for half of it," he said, and began to weep, and then began to weep with such intensity I thought he might vomit. I sat there feeling the shame of a parent who has punished her child too severely, or with humiliation instead of love. I've seen Rachel cry the same way. We do not remember pain, we remember objective correlatives, like the greenness of new grass, a mother's dress, and we forget how deeply the innocent feel their hurt, and that they do not understand it, and that we were meant to protect them. Oh, for a guardian angel, oh for the palm of its hand.

Gordon went straight to the bookstore to return the books he had bought that evening. "Please," he must have begged, for the store had a no-refund policy, "they were an impulsive purchase and I just found out I'm going to need the money for something else."

The clerk said, "The best I can offer is credit toward another purchase."

So Gordon turned around and the first book he saw was a student's guide to Europe. He picked it up and thumbed through its pages; Florence, Paris, London, not knowing that each city, its food and accents, its old styles of architecture, would be an assault on his senses. On the streets of Europe, he would grow into himself.

"I'll exchange these two books for this one," Gordon said, and he tucked the student guidebook and Dick Whittington under his arm as if he was holding a cat.

Marie teaches design and stagecraft now. I teach courses in Twentieth-Century Women—Women Between the Two

World Wars; Women After WW II; Women After Vietnam. What is the achievement of commenting on what you had no part in creating? There are so many women missing: my mother, for instance. She died with a tube in her throat, a greenish mask on her face, her hair kept tight on her skull by sweat and her pillow. She stared into the corner of the ceiling above her bed as if there were an exit there. Esther was with her. Esther said, "Go ahead, Mom. You don't have to wait for the girls. You can let go." My mother finally stared into Esther's eyes, and Esther knew, and said, "I'm going down the hall for a cigarette. I'll be back in a few minutes." My mother only wanted to die alone. She died while Esther waited in the hall.

In my mother's remains, I found things her mother left her. A letter: "Dearest Daughter, I thought I should take this time to write. The snow is falling softly across the yard. The Joiners drove me home after Sunday school. Their boy gave me a Valentine that says, God is Love. . . ."

Gordon's mother is missing, too, cursed forever with an aching curiosity after driving him to the Guardian Angel Home and kissing him good-bye. How she must wonder what happened to him, what harm and hurt she caused. Does she hope that he will find her after all these years?

And I think of an old lady I knew who once got so angry with her husband, she picked up a hammer and nails and built a second story to their house with the help of a neighbor boy. The issues hardest to grasp, sometimes the one you fought the hardest for, are the first you let go of. Or, worse perhaps, you become your subject, and you exhaust it. The problems of the world come down to this: All that we can imagine is more than we want to know.

Not long before he died, Jake was in the hospital with yet another infection for which there was no cure. The nurse came in to give him his bath, and he turned to me and said, "Would you do it, Sara?"

I had never bathed a man before, had not touched a man since Gordon. The nurse handed me a plastic basin, thin hospital linen, a tiny bar of Ivory soap still in its wrapper. I wiped Jake once with soapy water, then changed the water and the washcloth, and washed him down again. He was a solid man reduced to flesh and bones; but he was a big-boned man, and until you touched him, you did not know that he was wasting away. I started crying, and he said, "Poor, sweet Sara, you don't have to go on." I leaned over and kissed him, from the knuckles of his vertebrae to the soles of his feet.

In his will, he left Rachel enough money for school and travel afterward. He left me a drawing by Cassatt, a woman ironing. Just a possession, he once said of it.

Gordon never came back to Chicago. I didn't think he would. At times, I have called the operator in distant cities and asked for listings in his name. If Rachel were to walk in and he was here, she would know him immediately. She would blush and avert her eyes; at the most, she would say hi, and then she would go into her room and play her guitar, secretly hoping the music she played would please him. You can break your heart on all that you can imagine, all that you can put out of your mind, all that you can know.

Occasionally, I feel the brush of cashmere, or silk, or only terry cloth against the nipple of my amputated breast. The ghostly sensation is as thin as paper and cuts as clean. Gordon is older now. The difference in our ages would be inconsequential. I imagine him here now. I imagine him touching my scar tissue without my having to ask; what had not seemed a part of me, his lips are making deep and erotic. He is whispering my name over and over, like snow blowing over the frozen edges of a lake. What he cannot make whole again, he will convince me doesn't matter.

ALLEN BARNETT's work has appeared in *The New Yorker, Men on Men II, Christopher Street, The Advocate*, and *Poets and Writers*. A recipient of a New York Foundation for the Arts fellowship and a writing fellowship at Columbia University, he lives in New York. *The Body and Its Dangers and Other Stories*, his first story collection, has been nominated for two Lambda Literary Awards and has received a special citation from the Ernest Hemingway Foundation.